...him that her skin prickle... really was a magician and cou... her mind, because his eyes narrowed, and to her shock and undeniable excitement he slowly lowered his head.

'Lanzo…?' Her heart was thudding so hard she was sure he must hear it.

'*Cara,*' he murmured silkily. He had wanted to kiss her all evening. Even though she had carefully avoided him for most of the party, his eyes had followed her around the room and he had found himself recalling with vivid clarity how soft her mouth had felt beneath his ten years ago. Now the sexual tension between them was so intense that the air seemed to quiver. Desire flared, white-hot, inside him, and his instincts told him that she felt the same burning awareness. Anticipation made his hand a little unsteady as he lifted it to smooth her hair back from her face.

Chantelle Shaw lives on the Kent coast, five minutes from the sea, and does much of her thinking about the characters in her books while walking on the beach. She's been an avid reader from an early age. Her schoolfriends used to hide their books when she visited—but Chantelle would retreat into her own world, and still writes stories in her head all the time. Chantelle has been blissfully married to her own tall, dark and very patient hero for over twenty years, and has six children. She began to read Mills & Boon® as a teenager, and throughout the years of being a stay-at-home mum to her brood found romantic fiction helped her to stay sane! She enjoys reading and writing about strong-willed, feisty women, and even stronger-willed sexy heroes. Chantelle is at her happiest when writing. She is particularly inspired while cooking dinner, which unfortunately results in a lot of culinary disasters! She also loves gardening, walking, and eating chocolate (followed by more walking!).

THE ULTIMATE RISK

BY
CHANTELLE SHAW

First published in Great Britain 2011
by Mills & Boon, an imprint of Harlequin (UK) Limited,
Eton House, 18-24 Paradise Road, Richmond, Surrey TW9 1SR

© Chantelle Shaw 2011

ISBN: 978 0 263 88657 3

Harlequin (UK) policy is to use papers that are natural, renewable
and recyclable products and made from wood grown in sustainable
forests. The logging and manufacturing process conform to the
legal environmental regulations of the country of origin.

Printed and bound in Spain
by Blackprint CPI, Barcelona

THE ULTIMATE RISK

CHAPTER ONE

Did every woman remember her first lover? Gina wondered.

Surely she was not the only woman to have felt her heart slam against her ribs when she had glanced across a crowded room and caught sight of the man she had once been madly in love with?

It was definitely Lanzo. Their brief affair had taken place ten years ago, but he was regarded as one of Europe's most sought-after bachelors. Photographs of him regularly featured in celebrity gossip magazines and he was instantly recognisable. She couldn't help staring at him, conscious of that same swooping sensation in the pit of her stomach that she had felt when she had been eighteen and utterly in awe of him.

Perhaps he felt her scrutiny? Her breath caught in her throat when he turned his head in her direction. For a few seconds their eyes met and held, before Gina quickly looked away and pretended to idly scan the other guests at the party.

The tranquillity of Poole Harbour, on England's south coast, had been shattered over the weekend by the staging of the international offshore powerboat racing championships. Generally regarded as the most extreme and dangerous of all watersports, powerboat racing had been going on all day far out in the bay. But this evening the engines were silent, and dozens of sleek, futuristic-looking powerboats were moored in the harbour, bobbing gently on the swell.

It was certainly a sport that attracted the beautiful people, Gina noted, as she glanced around the restaurant where the after-race party was being held. Glamorous promotional models—uniformly tanned, blonde, and sporting unnaturally large breasts and very short skirts—flocked around bronzed, over-loud male boat crews, the drivers and throttle-men, who between them sent their boats skimming over the waves at death-defying speeds.

She had never understood why anyone would choose to risk their life for fun, and she had taken no interest in the racing. The party was definitely not her scene, and she had only come because her old schoolfriend Alex had recently taken over as manager of the exclusive Di Cosimo restaurant, and had requested her moral support on his first big event.

Instead, it was she who was in need of support, Gina reflected ruefully. Her legs felt like jelly and her head was spinning—but she could not blame either on the one glass of champagne she had drunk.

She was so shocked to see Lanzo again. She hadn't realised he was still involved in powerboat racing, and it had not crossed her mind that he might attend the party. True, he owned the restaurant, but it was one of many around the world belonging to the Di Cosimo chain, and she had not expected Lanzo to be in Poole. She was unprepared for her reaction to him, for the way her stomach muscles clenched and the tiny hairs on her arms prickled when she studied his achingly familiar profile.

With his striking looks—olive-gold skin, classically sculpted features, and silky jet-black hair that showed no signs of grey, even though he must be in his mid-thirties by now—Lanzo di Cosimo looked like one of those impossibly handsome male models who featured in fashion magazines. Tall and powerfully built, his tailored black trousers emphasised his height, and his white shirt was of such fine silk that the hard ridges of his abdominal muscles and the shadow of his dark chest hairs were visible beneath the material.

But it was more than just looks, Gina thought, as she stared down at her empty glass and dragged oxygen into her lungs. Lanzo possessed a simmering sensual magnetism that demanded attention. Supremely self-assured and devastatingly sexy, he was impossible to ignore, and the women who thronged around him made no attempt to hide their fascination with him.

He was a billionaire playboy whose passion for dangerous sports matched his passion for leggy blondes—none of whom remained in his life for long before he exchanged them for another model. Ten years ago, Gina had never really understood what he had seen in her—an averagely attractive brunette. But at eighteen she had been too overwhelmed by his interest to question it, and only later had realised that her attraction had probably been her embarrassingly puppy-like eagerness. Lanzo had not had to try very hard to persuade her into his bed, she acknowledged ruefully. For him she had been a convenient bedmate that summer he had spent in Poole, and no doubt he hadn't meant to break her heart—she only had herself to blame for that.

But time and maturity had healed the wounds of first love, she reminded herself. She was no longer the rather naïve girl with a massive crush on him she had been a decade ago. Resisting the urge to glance over at Lanzo again, she turned her back on him and strolled over to the huge wall of windows that ran the length of the restaurant and offered wonderful views over the harbour.

* * *

Lanzo shifted his position slightly so that he could continue to watch the woman in the blue dress who had caught his attention. He recognised her, but to his frustration could not place her. Now that she had her back to him he saw that her gleaming brown hair fell almost to her waist, and he imagined threading his fingers through the silky mass. Perhaps he had noticed her because she was so different from the blonde groupies who always attended the after-race parties, he mused, feeling a flicker of irritation when the young woman at his side, sensing that he was distracted, moved closer and deliberately pressed her nubile body up against him.

The girl *was* young, he thought with a frown as he glanced at her face, which would be far prettier without the thick layer of make-up. In her thigh-high skirt and ridiculous heels she reminded him of a baby giraffe—all gangly legs and long eyelashes. He doubted she was much over eighteen, but the invitation in her eyes told him he could bed her if he chose to. Once he would have been tempted, he acknowledged. But he was no longer a testosterone-fuelled twenty-year-old; his tastes had become more selective over the years, and he had no interest in girls barely out of high school.

'Congratulations on winning the race,' the blonde said breathlessly. 'I think powerboat racing is so exciting. How fast do you go?'

Lanzo stifled his impatience. 'The boat can reach a top speed of one hundred miles an hour.'

'Wow!' She smiled at him guilelessly. 'I'd love to go for a ride some time.'

He winced at the idea of giving 'rides' in his pride and joy. *The Falcon* was a million pounds' worth of superlative marine engineering. 'Racing boats are not ideal for sightseeing trips because they are built for speed rather than passenger comfort,' he explained. 'You would have more fun on a cruiser. I'll speak to a friend of mine and see if he'll take you on a trip along the coast,' he murmured, as he gently but firmly prised the girl's hand from his arm and moved away from her.

Gina watched the setting sun cast golden rays across the sea and gild the tops of the trees over on Brownsea Island. It was good to be home, she mused. She had spent most of the last ten years living and working in London, and she had forgotten how peaceful it was here on the coast.

But thinking about home, and more specifically her new, ultra-modern flat with its sea views, a little way along the quay, filled her with anxiety rather than pleasure. Since she had lost her job with a local company she had been unable to keep up with the mortgage repayments. The situation was horribly similar to the time when she had struggled to pay the mortgage and bills on the house she and Simon had owned in London, after he had lost his job and she had become the only wage earner.

After she had left him the house had been sold, but because it had been in negative equity she had come away with nothing. She had no savings—hence the reason why she had taken out such a large mortgage to buy the flat. But now it looked increasingly as though her only option was to sell her new home before the bank repossessed it.

Her life wasn't turning out the way she had planned it, she thought dismally. She had always assumed that a few years spent building her career would be followed by marriage and two children—a boy and a girl called Matthew and Charlotte. Well, she'd had the career, and she'd had the marriage, but she had learned that babies didn't arrive to order, however much you wanted them, and that marriages didn't always last, however hard you tried to make them work.

Her hand strayed unconsciously to the long, thin scar that ran down her cheek close to her ear, and continued down her neck, and she gave a little shiver. She had never expected that at twenty-eight she would be divorced, unemployed and seemingly infertile—the last evoked a familiar hollow ache inside her. Her grand life-plan had fallen apart, and now the prospect of losing the flat that she had bought when she had moved back to Poole, in the hope of starting a new life away from the bitter memories of her failed marriage, was the final straw.

Lost in her thoughts, she jumped when a voice sounded close to her ear.

'How do you think it's going?' Alex asked tensely. 'Do you think there's enough choice of canapés? I asked the chef to prepare twelve different types, including three vegetarian options.'

'It's a great party,' Gina assured him, pushing her concerns to the back of her mind and smiling at Alex. 'Stop looking so worried. You're too young for grey hairs.'

Alex gave a rueful laugh. 'I reckon I've gained a few since I took over as manager here. Lanzo di Cosimo demands the highest standards at all his restaurants, and it's important that I impress him tonight.'

'Well, I think you've done a brilliant job. Everything is great and the guests seem perfectly happy.' Gina paused, and then said in a carefully casual tone, 'I didn't realise that the head of Di Cosimo Holdings would be here.'

'Oh, yeah. Lanzo visits Poole two or three times a year. If you had come home more often instead of living it up in London, you would probably have seen him around,' Alex teased. 'He comes mainly for the powerboat racing, and a

year or so ago he bought a fabulous house on Sandbanks.'
He grinned. 'It's amazing to think that a little strip of sand
in Dorset is one of the most expensive places in the world to
live.' He suddenly stiffened. 'Speaking of the devil—here
he comes now,' he muttered below his breath.

Glancing over Alex's shoulder, Gina felt her stomach
lurch when she saw Lanzo striding in their direction. It
didn't matter how firmly she reminded herself that she was
a mature adult now, and well and truly over him. Her heart
was pounding and she felt as awkward and self-conscious
as she had been when she'd had a summer job as a waitress
in this very restaurant ten years ago.

His eyes were hypnotic—perhaps because their colour
was so unexpected, she thought shakily, her gaze drawn
against her will to his face. With his swarthy complexion
and jet-black hair, brown eyes would have seemed more
likely, but his irises were a startling vivid green, fringed
with thick black lashes and set beneath heavy brows.

Time had done the impossible and improved on perfection, Gina decided. At twenty-five, Lanzo had been a
sleek, incredibly handsome man who had still retained a
boyish air. A decade later he was rugged, sexy, and utterly gorgeous—his face all angles and planes, his slashing
cheekbones and square jaw softened by a mouth that was
full-lipped and blatantly sensual.

Something stirred inside her—something that went
deeper than sexual attraction. Although her physical reaction to him *was* shockingly intense, she acknowledged,
flushing when she saw Lanzo lower his gaze to the outline
of her nipples, clearly visible beneath her dress.

A long time ago he had held her in his arms and she had
felt certain that he was the only man in the world for her.
So many things had happened since then. She had escaped
from a violent marriage and knew that she was strong and

could look after herself. But for a crazy moment she wished Lanzo would draw her close against his broad chest and make her feel safe and *cherished*, as he had made her feel all those years ago.

But of course Lanzo had never really cherished her, she reminded herself sharply. It had just been an illusion—part of a silly daydream that he would fall in love with her as she had fallen in love with him. And, like most daydreams, it had turned to dust.

'The party is superb, Alex.' Lanzo greeted his restaurant manager, his eyes still focused on the woman at Alex's side. 'The food is excellent—as people expect from a Di Cosimo restaurant, of course.'

Alex visibly relaxed. 'Thank you. I'm glad you approve.' He suddenly realised that he did not have Lanzo's full attention, and gestured to Gina. 'Allow me to introduce a good friend of mine—Ginevra Bailey.'

'Ginevra—an Italian name,' Lanzo observed softly. He was intrigued by her obvious reluctance to shake his hand, and the slight tremble of her fingers when she placed them in his palm. Her skin was soft and pale, in stark contrast to his deep tan, and he had a sudden erotic image of her naked—of milky-white limbs entwined with his darker ones. He lifted her hand to his mouth and grazed his lips across her knuckles, feeling an unexpectedly sharp tug of desire in his gut when her eyes widened and darkened.

Gina snatched her hand from Lanzo's grasp, feeling as though an electrical current had shot along her arm. She swallowed and struggled for composure. 'My grandmother was Italian, and I was given her name,' she murmured coolly, thankful that the years she had spent working for the very demanding chairman of a world-renowned department store chain meant that she was an expert at hiding her private thoughts. Hopefully no one would guess that

Lanzo's close proximity was making her heart race so fast
that she felt breathless and churned up inside.

His green eyes glittered and she quickly looked away
from him, assuring herself that he could not possibly read
her mind. He gave a small frown as he studied her intently.
She sensed that he was intrigued by her, but she had no
intention of reminding him that they had once, very briefly,
been lovers. Ten years was a long time, and undoubtedly
countless other women had shared his bed since her. It was
far better, and less embarrassing, that he did not recognise
her. And, to be fair, it was not his fault that, while she had
not forgotten him, he had presumably never given her a
second thought after he had casually announced at the end
of that summer a decade ago that he was returning to his
home in Italy.

Lanzo's eyes narrowed as he studied Ginevra Bailey.
Something about her tugged on his mind, but the faint
memory was elusive. And as he skimmed his gaze over
her hourglass figure, displayed to perfection by a navy blue
silk-jersey dress that clung to her curves, he was certain
that if they *had* met on a previous occasion he would not
have forgotten her.

Her beauty was understated: a perfect oval-shaped face,
skin as smooth as porcelain, and deep blue eyes that were
almost the exact shade of her dress. Once again something
stirred in his subconscious—a distant recollection of eyes
as intensely blue as the deep ocean—but the memory remained frustratingly intangible, and perhaps it was nothing.
He had known many women, he acknowledged wryly. It
was possible that Ginevra Bailey simply reminded him of
a past mistress whose identity eluded him.

Beside him, Alex made a slight movement, and Lanzo
realised with a jolt that he was staring at the beautiful brunette. He resisted the temptation to reach out and run his

fingers through the long chestnut-brown hair that rippled down her back and inhaled sharply, his body taut with sexual anticipation. He had not been so instantly turned on for a long time, and his reaction was all the more surprising because he was usually attracted to tall, willowy blondes. The woman in front of him was a delectable package of voluptuous curves who was having a profound affect on his libido, and Lanzo was in no doubt that he intended to bed her at the first opportunity.

'I hope you are enjoying the party, Ginevra,' he murmured. 'Are you a fan of powerboat racing?'

'No. I've never seen the attraction of dangerous sports,' Gina replied shortly.

She was struggling to disguise her overwhelming awareness of Lanzo, and must have sounded more abrupt than she had intended because Alex interspersed quickly, 'Gina was responsible for the floral displays tonight. The table centrepieces are beautiful, don't you think?'

'Indeed.' Lanzo glanced at the arrangement of red and white roses and trailing variegated ivy on a nearby table. 'You are a florist then…Gina?' He frowned, wondering why the shortened version of her name seemed familiar.

'Not professionally. It's simply a hobby,' she replied. During her marriage to Simon he had encouraged her to take an expensive flower-arranging course, as well as an even more expensive course of lessons in French cuisine, so that she could be the perfect hostess at his business dinner parties. The cookery lessons were not of much use now that she was only preparing meals for herself—often a ready-meal heated up in the microwave, Gina thought ruefully—but she had enjoyed making the floral displays for the party.

'The floristry firm I'd originally booked were forced to pull out because of staff illness,' Alex explained. 'Luckily

Gina offered to step in and decorate the tables.' He paused as he caught sight of one of the waiters frantically signalling to him from across the room. 'There seems to be some sort of crisis in the kitchen,' he muttered. 'Would you excuse me?'

Gina watched Alex thread his way through the throng of guests, feeling a flutter of tension now that she was alone with Lanzo. Of course they were not really alone, she reminded herself impatiently. The restaurant was packed with party guests, but as she slowly turned back to him she felt the strangest sensation that they were in a bubble, distanced somehow from the hum of voices around them.

Surely every woman remembered her first lover? she told herself again. Her response to Lanzo was a natural reaction to seeing a face from the past. But deep down she knew it was more than that. She'd had a couple of relationships before she had married, but no other man—not even Simon in the happier times of their marriage—had evoked this helpless, out-of-control longing; this violent, almost primitive desire that shocked her with its intensity.

Lanzo had been incredibly special to her, she acknowledged. Although their affair had not lasted long, the discovery that a man like him—an international jet-set playboy who could have any woman he wanted—had desired her, had boosted her confidence. Because of him she had changed from a shy teenager into a self-assured woman who had built a successful career and later caught the eye of an equally successful City banker.

But if Lanzo had given her confidence Simon had stripped it from her, she thought ruefully. Thanks to her disastrous marriage she no longer had faith in her judgement of others. She felt stupid that she had not realised what Simon was really like beneath his charming exterior, and right now she was wary of Lanzo's potent masculinity and felt painfully vulnerable.

To her relief a waiter approached and offered to refill her glass. Usually she only had one drink at social events—a throwback to all the times Simon had drunk too much at parties and become embarrassingly loud and unpleasant. But tonight she was grateful for any distraction from Lanzo's overwhelming presence, and when the waiter had gone and she was alone with him once more she took a hurried sip of her champagne and felt the bubbles explode on her tongue.

'So you don't like powerboat racing?' he drawled, in his gravelly, sexy accent. 'Are there any forms of watersports you *do* like?'

'I enjoyed learning to sail in the bay when I was a child. Sailing is rather more peaceful than tearing through the water at a ridiculous speed,' she said pointedly.

'But not as adrenalin-pumping,' Lanzo murmured, his eyes glinting with amusement when she blushed.

Gina had a horrible feeling that he knew her adrenalin levels were sky-high as her instincts sensed the threat he posed to her peace of mind and she prepared to fight him or flee.

'Do you live locally, Gina?' The way he curled his tongue around her name caused needle-darts of pleasure to shiver across her skin.

'Yes, I was born here. Actually, I'm the fourth generation of Baileys to be born in Poole—but the last, I'm afraid, because I don't have any brothers to carry on the family name.' She knew she was babbling but it was preferable to an awkward silence, when Lanzo might hear the loud thudding of her heart. She took a deep breath and prayed that her usual calm nature would reassert itself. 'Are you staying in Poole for long, Signor di Cosimo?'

'Lanzo,' he corrected her. 'Regrettably, this is only a short trip as I have other business commitments, but I hope to return soon.' He studied her flushed face and smiled. 'Perhaps sooner than I had planned,' he drawled.

Gina felt trapped by a powerful force that would not allow her to tear her eyes from Lanzo's face. They were alone in a room full of people, bound together by a powerful chemistry that held them both in its thrall.

Lanzo watched her pupils widen until her eyes were deep, dark pools, and his body tautened as heat surged through his veins. She had intrigued him from the moment he had glanced across the room and discovered her watching him. It happened to him all the time. Women had stared at him since he was a teenager. But never before had he felt such a strong urge to respond to the desire that darkened her eyes to the colour of midnight.

The loud smash of glass shattering on the tiled floor hurtled Gina back to reality, and she looked around to see that one of the waitresses had dropped a tray of glasses. She was shocked to realise how close she was standing to Lanzo and she jerked back from him, her face burning when she caught the hard gleam in his eyes. How long had she been staring at him like an over-awed teenager? she wondered, feeling hot with embarrassment. She had no recollection of either of them moving, but their bodies had been so close that her pelvis had almost brushed against his.

Tearing her gaze from him, she saw that the waitress was trying to gather up the shards of glass with her hands. 'I'll get a broom,' she muttered, and hurried across the restaurant, grateful for the chance to escape Lanzo's intent stare.

He watched her walk away from him, feeling himself harden as he studied the gentle sway of her bottom beneath its covering of tight navy silk.

Oh, Gina! What a transformation time had wrought, he mused, for he had suddenly solved the puzzle of why she seemed familiar. He remembered her now—although she looked very different from the shy waitress who had followed him around with puppy-dog devotion and been so sweetly anxious to please him that summer he had spent in England.

He had not known that her proper name was Ginevra. It suited the sophisticated woman she had become. And really it was not surprising that he had initially failed to recognise her, he assured himself, because this elegant woman, with her toned figure and her mane of glossy chestnut hair, bore scant resemblance to the slightly plump, awkward girl who had delighted him with her unexpectedly passionate nature when she had been his lover for a few weeks one summer, a long time ago.

Was the grown-up Gina still the sensual, uniquely generous lover who had appeared in his dreams for several months after he had returned to Italy? Lanzo brooded. Events in his life had taught him to live for the present and never revisit the past. But he was prepared to make an exception in this instance, he mused, watching her until she disappeared into the kitchens with a determined gleam in his eyes that would have worried her had she seen it.

CHAPTER TWO

IT STILL wasn't completely dark, even though it was almost eleven o'clock, Gina noted when she emerged from the restaurant and glanced up at the indigo sky which was studded with a few faint stars. The water in the harbour was flat and calm, and the salt tang carried on the breeze was a welcome contrast to the stifling atmosphere of the restaurant.

She loved the long days and balmy evenings of June, and she paused for a moment, enjoying the fresh air which was cool but did not require her to slip on her jacket, before she turned and began to stroll along the quay.

'I did not realise that you still lived in Poole.' A tall figure stepped out of the shadows, and Gina's heart skittered when Lanzo fell in step beside her. 'I visit several times a year and I'm surprised I haven't seen you around.'

Gina gave him a startled glance, her heart thudding with the realisation that he had finally recognised her. The expression in his eyes made her pulse quicken. It was the intense, predatory look of a panther stalking its prey, she thought, and then gave herself a mental shake. He was just a man, she reminded herself irritably. But the soft night air carried the spicy drift of his aftershave, and as her senses quivered she ruefully acknowledged that Lanzo would never be 'just' anything.

'Perhaps you did see me on one of your previous visits, but you didn't remember me,' she said tartly, still feeling faintly chagrined that he had not realised her identity back at the restaurant.

'Oh, I remember you, Gina,' he said softly. 'Although I admit I did not immediately recognise you tonight. You've changed a lot since I knew you.'

He wanted to run his fingers through her long silky hair, but he had noticed how she had tensed the moment she had seen him outside the restaurant. The flash of awareness in her deep blue eyes when she had first spotted him had told him that she was as conscious of the fierce sexual chemistry between them as he, but for some reason she seemed determined to ignore it.

'Your hair especially is different from the style you wore ten years ago,' he commented.

'Don't remind me,' Gina groaned, utterly mortified by the memory of the curly perm she had believed would make her look older and more sophisticated than the ponytail she'd had since she was six. The perm had been a disaster, which had transformed her hair into an untameable bush with the texture of wire wool, and rather than looking sexy and sophisticated she had resembled a chubby poodle. As if the perm hadn't been bad enough, she had been a few pounds overweight, she remembered grimly. 'I can't imagine why you ever noticed me,' she muttered.

In all honesty he had *not* taken much notice of her when he had first arrived in Poole to oversee the launch of the Di Cosimo restaurant here all those years ago, Lanzo remembered. Gina had simply been one of the staff—a part-time waitress who helped out with the washing up on nights when the restaurant was especially busy.

She had been a shy, mousy girl, with an annoying habit of looking at the floor whenever he spoke to her—until on one occasion he had been so irritated by her studious inspection of the carpet that he had cupped her chin in his hand and tilted her face upwards and had found himself staring into the bluest eyes he had ever seen.

The unremarkable waitress was not so ordinary after all, he had been amazed to discover, as he had studied her flawless peaches-and-cream complexion and her wide, surprisingly kissable mouth. He could not remember their conversation—it had probably been something inconsequential, like asking her to fill the salt-cellars—but after that he had noticed her more often, and had invariably found her watching him. Although she had blushed scarlet and hastily looked away whenever he had met her gaze.

That summer ten years ago had been a dark period in his life, Lanzo reflected grimly. Alfredo had died in the spring, and he had been struggling to come to terms with the loss of the man he had regarded as a second father—the man who would have been his father-in-law had it not been for the devastating fire that had swept through the di Cosimo family home and taken the lives of Lanzo's parents and his fiancée five years before that.

Cristina's face was a distant memory now—like a slightly out of focus photograph—and the pain of her loss no longer felt like a knife being thrust through his heart. But he remembered her; he would always remember the gentle girl he had fallen in love with all those years ago.

Widower Alfredo and Lanzo's parents had been delighted when he had announced that Cristina had agreed to be his wife. But a week before the wedding tragedy had struck.

The familiar feeling of guilt made Lanzo's gut clench, and he stared out across the harbour to where the darkening sky met the sea, lost in black memories. He should not have gone on that business trip to Sweden. Cristina had begged him not to, saying that they needed to talk. But he had been shocked by her revelation that she was pregnant—so unprepared for the prospect of having a child when they had both decided that they would wait at least five years before they started a family.

He had been so young—only twenty—and determined to make his father proud of him as he took on more responsibilities at Di Cosimo Holdings. But that was no excuse, he thought grimly. He'd known Cristina had been hurt by his lack of enthusiasm for the baby. He hadn't wanted to talk about it, and instead had insisted on going on the business trip when he had known full well that he could have sent one of his staff in his place. But he had wanted time alone, to get his head around the idea of being a father, and so he had ignored Cristina's tears and flown to Sweden.

Within twenty-four hours he had realised that he had behaved like an idiot. He loved Cristina, and of course he would love their child. He had been impatient to get home and convince her that he was delighted about the baby, but his meeting had overrun, meaning that he had missed his flight, and he'd had to spend another night away. The following morning he had arrived in Italy and been met by Alfredo, who had broken the devastating news that his parents and Cristina had all died in the fire that had destroyed the di Cosimo villa.

Lanzo's jaw tightened as he remembered the agony of that moment—the feeling that his heart had been ripped from his chest. He had not told Alfredo that Cristina had been a few weeks pregnant. The older man had been utterly distraught at the loss of his only daughter and there had seemed little point in making his grief worse. But the bitter truth was that he could not bear anyone to know how he had failed his fiancée and his unborn child, Lanzo acknowledged. He should never have gone away. Cristina had died believing that he did not want their child, and he had never been able to forgive himself for not being with her when she had needed him most.

Alfredo had never got over losing his daughter, but the older man had become an invaluable father figure and advisor, for with his own father gone Lanzo had become the head of Di Cosimo Holdings at the age of twenty. Five years later Alfredo's death had hit him hard, but he had dealt with it as he had dealt with the loss of Cristina and his parents—by burying his grief deep in his heart.

The opening of a new restaurant in England had given him an excuse to spend some time away from Italy and his memories. He had thrown himself into work, and into offshore powerboat racing, which was a popular sport along the south coast. It had satisfied a need in him to push himself to his limits and beyond. He'd loved the speed, the danger and the adrenalin rush, the idea that death was one flip of the boat away—for deep down he had not really cared what happened to him. Subconsciously he had hoped that one day he would push himself too far and death would take him, as it had Cristina. But for fifteen years he had cheated death and been left alone to bear his grief. Sometimes he wondered if it was his punishment for those first doubts he'd had about being a father.

'I noticed you,' he told Gina abruptly. She had been a calming influence on his crazy mood that summer—a nondescript girl with a gentle smile that had soothed his troubled soul.

For the first two years after Cristina's death he had not looked at another woman, and when he had finally started dating again his relationships had been meaningless sexual encounters. He had closed the door on his emotions and deliberately chosen mistresses who accepted his terms. But Gina had been different. Something about her youthful enthusiasm had reminded him of the carefree days of his own youth—a time that seemed bathed in perpetual sunshine before the black cloak of grief had settled on his shoulders. When he'd been with Gina his mood had lightened, and he had enjoyed spending time with her. It had only been when he had found himself thinking about asking her to return to Italy with him that he had realised there was a danger she was starting to mean something to him—and he had immediately ended their affair. For he associated love with pain, and he never wanted to experience either emotion ever again.

'You were sweet and shy, and you used to stare at me when you thought I didn't notice,' he said gruffly. She had seemed painfully innocent, although she had assured him that she'd had several boyfriends, Lanzo recalled.

Sweet was such an unflattering description. It conjured an image of a silly lovesick teenager—which of course was exactly what she had been ten years ago, Gina thought ruefully. She remembered how her heart had thudded with excitement whenever Lanzo had been around—rather like it was doing now, a little voice in her head taunted. But the difference now was that she was a confident career woman—albeit one without a career at the moment—and she was perfectly in control of her emotions.

'I admit I had an outsize crush on you,' she said lightly. 'But it was hardly surprising when I'd attended an all-girls school and had little contact with the male species—especially the exotic Italian variety.'

'Why didn't you remind me tonight that we knew each other?' Lanzo asked her curiously.

She shrugged. 'Because it was a long time ago, and I barely remembered you.'

His mocking smile told her he knew she was lying, and she was thankful that it was probably too dark now for him to notice her blush. They had reached the attractive block of six flats on the quayside where she lived, and as she slowed her steps he halted in front of her.

'But you did not forget me completely during the past ten years,' he stated arrogantly, his deep, velvety voice sending a little quiver down Gina's spine. 'Are you cold?' he asked, noticing the tremor that ran through her.

'Yes,' she lied again, 'but I live here. Well,' she said briskly, desperate to get away from him before she made a complete idiot of herself, 'it's been nice to meet you again.'

She stepped back from him, but instead of bidding her goodnight he smiled and moved closer, so that they were enclosed in the shadowed porch area in front of the flats.

'You can't have lived here long. These flats were still under construction when I was here last year,' he commented.

'I moved here from London four months ago.'

'That must have been a big change,' Lanzo murmured, glancing over his shoulder at the fishing boats moored in the harbour.

Gina nodded. 'I worked in the City and I'd forgotten how quiet it is here.'

'What job do you do? I assume you have moved on from waiting tables?' he said, his eyes glinting as he allowed them to roam over her navy silk dress and matching stiletto-heeled sandals. It was impossible to equate this elegant woman with the curly-haired young waitress from ten year ago.

'Until recently I was PA to the chairman of the Meyers chain of department stores.'

He looked impressed. 'That's certainly a long way from waitressing. Meyers have outlets in virtually every major city around the world. But surely you don't commute to the City from here every day?'

'No, I decided to leave the company when my boss retired. There were a number of reasons why I wanted to move out of London.' Not least the late-night abusive phone calls from her ex-husband, Gina thought grimly. 'My father suffered a heart attack at Christmas. He's recovered well, thankfully, but I decided to move closer to my family. Dad's illness brought it home to me that you never know what the future holds.'

'Very true,' Lanzo said in a curiously flat tone. Gina gave him a curious glance, but his expression was unfathomable. 'Too often we take the people we care about for granted.'

She nodded. 'I came back to Poole to work as the PA for the head of a construction company. Unfortunately the market for new houses has been hit by the recession, and Hartman Homes went into liquidation last month. I've been looking for a new job, but there's not a lot around. The way things are going I might need to take up waitressing again,' she quipped, trying to quell the familiar flare of panic that thoughts of her precarious finances induced.

'Come and see me at the restaurant in the morning. I may be able to help you,' Lanzo murmured.

She gave him a startled glance. 'I was joking about being a waitress,' she told him, privately thinking that she would consider almost any job in order to keep up with her mortgage repayments.

'I'm serious. I urgently need a personal assistant to fill in for my usual PA while she is on maternity leave. Luisa had planned to work up until her baby was born, but she has high blood pressure and has been advised to give up work early. Her absence is causing me all sorts of problems,'

Lanzo added, sounding distinctly unsympathetic for his secretary.

'High blood pressure can be dangerous for an expectant mother and her unborn child,' Gina told him. 'I'm not surprised your PA has been told to take things easy. She couldn't have travelled with you in the later stages of her pregnancy anyway. Pregnant women shouldn't fly after about thirty-six weeks.'

'Shouldn't they?' Lanzo shrugged. 'I admit I know little about pregnancy—it is not something that interests me.' He had never come to terms with his belief that he had failed his unborn baby, and he had vowed never to have another child. 'But you seem very knowledgeable on the subject.' He frowned as a thought struck him. 'Do you have a child?'

'No,' she said shortly. Since she had moved back to Poole she had met several of her old schoolfriends, pushing prams around the town, and invariably the question of whether she had children had cropped up. The answer always hurt, Gina acknowledged, however much she laughed and made the excuse that she had been too busy with her career, and there was plenty of time for babies.

'Some of my friends and both my stepsisters have children, so obviously I've picked up a few facts about pregnancy. I hope your PA keeps well in the final weeks before her baby is born,' she murmured, feeling a sharp pang of sadness that every woman but her, it seemed, had no problem conceiving a child.

That wasn't true, she reminded herself. Endometriosis was a well-known cause of female infertility, although for years she hadn't realised that her heavy and painful periods were an indication of a medical condition that could affect her chances of having a baby.

Her gynaecologist had explained that there were various

treatments available that might help her conceive, but he had emphasised that to maximise her chances she should try to fall pregnant before she reached her thirties. As a recently divorced twenty-eight-year-old, she had been forced to face the heartbreaking fact that she might never be a mother, Gina acknowledged bleakly.

'Where have you gone?'

Lanzo's voice tugged her from her thoughts and she stared at him helplessly. Seeing him tonight had taken her back in time. Life had been so optimistic and so full of exciting possibilities when she had been eighteen, but the last few years especially had been chequered with disappointments, she thought sadly.

That summer she had spent with Lanzo was a golden memory she had treasured, and even the misery she had felt after he had returned to Italy had served a purpose. Desperate to put him out of her mind, she had decided to move away from Poole, where it had seemed that every street and quaint country pub held memories of the few weeks they had spent together, and instead of accepting a place at nearby Bournemouth University she had taken a secretarial course, moved to London, and forged a highly successful career.

But Lanzo had been right when he had guessed that she had never forgotten him. Oh, she'd got over him—after a while. She had grown up and moved on, and he had faded to the background of her new, busy life. But occasionally she had found herself thinking about him, and curiously it had been Lanzo, not Simon, she had dreamed about on the night before her wedding. Now, unbelievably, he was here, watching her with an intense expression in his mesmeric green eyes that made her heart-rate quicken.

'I...I really must go in,' she said faintly.

His slow smile stole her breath. 'Why?'

'Well…' She searched her blank mind for a good reason. 'It's getting late. I should get to bed…' She cringed. Why had she used *that* word? She had been fighting her memories of his toned, tanned, naked body—of his hands gently pushing her thighs apart so that he could sink between them. She felt the hot throb of desire low in her pelvis and closed her eyes, as if blotting him from her vision would free her from his sorcery.

'Stay and talk to me for a while,' he said softly. 'It's good to see you again, Gina.'

His words were beguiling. Her eyes flew open. It was good to see him too, she acknowledged silently. During the last grim months of her marriage and her subsequent divorce she had felt as though she were trapped in a long dark tunnel. But the unexpectedness of seeing Lanzo again made her feel as though the sun had emerged from behind a storm cloud and was warming her with its golden rays.

Her blue eyes clashed with his glinting gaze. She did not want to talk, she admitted shakily. She was so aware of him that her skin prickled, and her nipples felt as hard as pebbles, straining against the constriction of her bra. Perhaps he really was a magician and could read her mind. Because his eyes had narrowed, and to her shock and undeniable excitement he slowly lowered his head.

'Lanzo…?' Her heart was thudding so hard she was sure he must hear it.

'Cara,' he murmured silkily. He had wanted to kiss her all evening. Even though she had carefully avoided him for the rest of the party after she had gone to report the broken glass to the restaurant manager, his eyes had followed her around the room and he had found himself recalling with vivid clarity how soft her mouth had felt beneath his ten years ago. Now the sexual tension between them was so intense that the air seemed to quiver. Desire flared, white-

hot, inside him, and his instincts told him that she felt the same burning awareness. Anticipation made his hand a little unsteady as he lifted it to smooth her hair back from her face.

Gina stiffened at Lanzo's touch and instinctively jerked her head back. She had concealed her scar with make-up, but she was mortified to think that he might feel the distinct ridge that ran down her cheek and neck.

'Don't.' The plea left her lips before she could stop it. She flushed when his brows rose quizzically. He had every right to look surprised, she thought miserably. Seconds ago she had been leaning close to him, waiting to feel the first brush of his mouth over hers. But when he had touched her face she had been catapulted from her dream-like state back to reality.

She could not bear to see the desire in his eyes turn to revulsion—as would surely happen if he saw her scar. Even worse would be his curiosity. What if he asked her how she had been injured? Nothing would induce her to make the humiliating admission that her ex-husband was respon-sible for the unsightly scar that now served as a physical reminder of her gullibility.

It sickened her to think that once she had believed she loved Simon, and that he loved her. Only after their wed-ding had she realised that she had not known the true nature of the man, who had hidden his unpredictable temper be-neath a charming façade. She felt ashamed that she had been taken in by Simon, and had sworn that she would never be so trusting again. What did she really know of Lanzo? her brain questioned. Her heart had leapt in recog-nition when she had first seen him tonight, and all evening she had been swamped with memories of their affair, but in truth her relationship with him ten years ago had lasted for a matter of weeks and he was virtually a stranger.

Lanzo's eyes narrowed as he watched Gina physically and mentally withdraw from him, and for a few seconds a mixture of anger and frustration flared inside him. She had wanted him to kiss her. He knew he had not imagined the desire that had darkened her eyes to sapphire pools. So why had she pulled back?

The young Gina of his memories had been open and honest, and she had responded to him with an eagerness that he had found curiously touching. It appeared that the more mature, sophisticated Gina had learned to play the games that so many women played, he thought grimly. He had had mistresses in the past who had calculated his wealth and made it clear that their sexual favours came at a price: jewellery, designer clothes, perhaps being set up in a luxury apartment. He presumed that Gina was no different, but he was surprised by the strength of his disappointment.

He stepped back from her and gave her a cool smile. 'I was wondering if you would like to have dinner with me at my house on Sandbanks?'

The address was a sure-fire winner—reputed to be the fourth most expensive place in the world to live. He had never met a woman yet who had not known that properties on that exclusive part of the Dorset coast were mostly worth in excess of ten million pounds. No doubt Gina would be rather more willing to kiss him now that she realised quite how loaded he was, he thought sardonically.

Lanzo had issued his invitation in a perfectly polite tone, but something in his voice made Gina glad that she had not allowed him to kiss her. The warmth had faded from his eyes, and as she met his hard, glinting green gaze a little shiver ran though her. He was a stranger, her brain reiterated, and there was no reason why she should trust him.

She forced her own polite smile. 'That's very kind of you, but I'm afraid I'm busy every day next week—and as you told me you are only in Poole for a short visit I doubt we will be able to fit dinner into our respective schedules.'

Lanzo stared at Gina in astonishment, hardly able to believe that she had turned him down. It had never happened to him before, and for a moment he was lost for words. He was used to the fact that his looks and wealth were a potent combination which guaranteed him female attention wherever he went. He only had to click his fingers to have any woman who caught his eye. Ten years ago he had recognised that Gina had had a crush on him. She had fallen into his bed with little effort on his part, and if he was honest he had confidently assumed that she would do so again.

But it was not only her appearance that had changed, he mused. At eighteen she had been shy at first with him, but when he had got to know her and she had relaxed with him he had been charmed by her love of life and her cheerful, carefree nature. At that black period of his life she had seemed like a breath of fresh air, and a welcome distraction from the grim memories of his past.

What had happened in the ten years since he had last seen Gina that had robbed her of her youthful exuberance? he wondered. The woman standing before him had appeared sophisticated and self-assured at the party, but now that they were alone she was tense and on edge, watching him warily—as if she expected him to do what…? he wondered with a frown. *Dio,* she was afraid of him, he suddenly realised. She had not pulled away from him because she was playing the coquette, but because she did not trust him.

Outrage caused him to stiffen. What in heaven's name had he done to make her think he might harm her in some way? Following swiftly on the heels of that thought came the realisation that something, or *someone*, from her past must have caused her to change from a fun-loving girl to a woman who was desperately trying to disguise the fact that she was nervous of him. He wanted to ask her *who*? *What* had happened to her that made her flinch from him?

He looked at her tense face and acknowledged that she was not likely to confide in him. More surprising was the feeling of protectiveness that swept through him—together with anger that someone had turned her from the trusting, happy girl he had once known to a woman who was wary and mistrustful, with an air of sadness about her that tugged on his insides.

'What a busy life you must lead if you do not have one free night,' he murmured. 'Perhaps we can postpone my invitation to dinner until my next visit to Poole?' he added softly when she blushed. He held out his hand. 'Give me your key.'

'Why?' Gina could not hide the suspicion in her voice. What did he want? Was he hoping she would invite him in for coffee, and then expect the invitation to lead to something more? Panic churned inside her. Since her divorce she had been on a couple of dinner dates, but she had never been alone with a man. Simon had caused untold damage to her self-confidence, she acknowledged heavily. She wanted to move on, have other relationships and maybe even fall in love, but sometimes she despaired that she would ever be able to trust a man again.

'I was merely going to see you safely inside,' Lanzo explained steadily, taking the key that Gina was clutching in her fingers.

He stood staring down at her for a few moments, and her breath caught in her throat when something flared in his eyes. She wondered if he was going to ignore her earlier plea and kiss her after all, and she realised that part of her wished he would pull her into his arms and slant his sensual mouth over hers. She wanted to forget Simon's cruelty and lose herself in Lanzo's potent magnetism. Unconsciously she moistened her lower lip with the tip of her tongue, and heard his swiftly indrawn breath.

'*Buona notte*, Gina,' he said quietly, and then, to her shock, he turned and walked away, striding along the quay without a single glance over his shoulder. His tall, broad-shouldered figure was gradually swallowed up by the darkness, and the ring of his footsteps faded into the night, leaving her feeling strangely bereft.

For a few moments she stared after him, and then stepped into her flat and shut the door, realising as she did so that she had been holding her breath. Why on earth, she asked herself angrily, did she feel an overwhelming urge to burst into tears? Was it the thought that she would probably never see Lanzo again after she had refused his invitation to dinner? He was a billionaire playboy who could have any woman he wanted and he was not likely to bother with her again.

She was too wound up to go to bed, and after flicking through the TV channels and finding nothing that captured her attention she headed for the bathroom and ran a bath. Lanzo's darkly handsome face filled her consciousness, and with a sigh she sank into the fragrant bubbles and allowed her mind to drift back ten years.

She had been so excited to be offered a job as a waitress at the swanky new Italian restaurant on the quay, Gina recalled. She'd just finished her A-levels and been desperate to earn some money to spend on new summer clothes. While she had been at school she had received a small allowance from her father, but the family farm barely made a profit and money had always been tight.

Lanzo had arrived in Poole for the opening night of the

Di Cosimo restaurant and stayed for the summer. Golden-skinned, exotic, and heart-stoppingly sexy, he had been so far removed from the few boys of her own age Gina had dated that she had been blown away by his stunning looks and lazy charm.

He had a reputation as a playboy, and he'd always had a gorgeous woman clinging to his arm. How she had envied those women, Gina remembered ruefully. How she had longed to be beautiful and blonde and thin. But Lanzo had never seemed to notice her—until one day he had spoken to her and she had been so tongue-tied that she had stared at the floor, praying he would not notice her scarlet face.

'Don't slouch,' he had instructed her. 'You should hold your head up and be confident—not scurry around like a little mouse. When you look down no one can see your eyes, which is a pity because you have beautiful eyes,' he had added slowly, and he had tilted her chin and stared down at her.

She had hardly been able to breathe, and when he had smiled she had practically melted at his feet and smiled shyly back at him. And that had been the start, she thought. From that day Lanzo had made a point of saying hello to her, or bidding her goodnight at the end of her shift. When he had learned that she had to race out of the restaurant when it closed so that she could catch the last bus home he had insisted on driving her back to the farm, and those journeys in his sports car had become the highlight of her days.

Lanzo drove at a hair-raising speed, and that first night Gina had gripped her seat as they had hurtled down the narrow country lanes, the hedgerows flashing past in a blur.

'Relax—I'm a good driver,' he had said in an amused voice. 'Tell me about yourself.'

That had certainly made her forget her fear that he would misjudge the next sharp bend and they would crash. What on earth was there to tell? She'd been sure the mundane details of her life would be of no interest to a playboy billionaire, but she had obediently chatted to him about growing up on the farm with her father and stepmother, and her two stepsisters.

'My parents divorced when I was eight, and when Dad married Linda a few years later she brought her daughters, Hazel and Sarah, to live at the farm.'

'What about your mother?' Lanzo asked. 'Why didn't you live with her after the divorce?'

'Dad thought it would be better for me to stay with him. My mother had been having an affair behind my father's back, and one day I came home from school to find a note saying she had left us for one of the labourers Dad had employed on the farm. Mum never stayed in one place for long, or with one man,' Gina admitted. 'I visited her occasionally, but I was happier living with Dad and Linda.'

Witnessing her mother's chaotic lifestyle and her numerous volatile relationships had made Gina realise that she wanted her future to be very different. Marriage, a happy home and children might not be fashionable goals, but she wasn't ashamed to admit that they were more important to her than a high-flying career.

Lanzo drove her home several times a week, and she slowly grew more relaxed with him—although her intense awareness of him never lessened. He was always charming, but sometimes she sensed a dark mood beneath his smile. There was a restless tension about him, and an air of deep sadness that puzzled and disturbed her, but he never spoke of his personal life and she was too shy to pry.

'I find you peaceful company, Gina,' he told her one night when he stopped the car outside the farm gates.

'Is that a polite way of saying I'm boring?' she blurted out, wishing with all her heart that he thought she was gorgeous and sexy. *Peaceful* made her sound like a nun.

'Of course not. I don't find you at all boring,' he assured her quietly. He turned his head towards her, and the brilliant gleam in his green eyes made Gina's heart lurch. 'You are very lovely,' he murmured deeply, before he brushed his mouth over hers in a kiss that was as soft as thistledown and left her yearning for more.

'I checked the rota and saw that it's your day off tomorrow. Would you like to come out with me on my boat?'

Would she?

She barely slept that night, and the next day when she heard Lanzo's car pull up on the drive she dashed out to meet him, her face pink with an excitement that at eighteen she was too young and naïve to try and disguise.

It had been a glorious day, Gina remembered, sliding deeper beneath the bathwater. The sun had shone from a cloudless blue sky as Lanzo had steered the luxurious motor cruiser he had chartered out of the harbour. His dark mood seemed to have disappeared, and he'd been charismatic and mouth-wateringly sexy, his faded jeans sitting low on his hips and his chest bared to reveal an impressive six-pack. Gina had watched him with a hungry yearning in her eyes, and her heart had raced when he had pulled her into his arms and kissed her.

They had cruised along the coast, picnicked in a secluded bay, and later he had made love to her in the cabin below deck. The sound of the waves lapping against the boat and the mewing cry of the gulls had mingled with his low murmurs of pleasure when he had stroked his hands over her trembling, eager body.

There had been one moment when her hesitancy had

made him pause. 'It's not your first time, is it?' he had
asked with a frown.

'No,' she'd lied, terrified that he would stop if she admitted the truth.

But he hadn't stopped. He had kissed her with a feverish
passion that had thrilled her, and caressed her with gentle,
probing fingers until she had been so aroused that when
he had finally entered her there had been no discomfort,
just a wonderful sense of completeness—as if she had been
waiting all her life for this moment and this man.

The bathwater had cooled, and Gina shivered as she
sat up abruptly and reached for a towel. She had not only
give Lanzo her virginity that day, she had given him her
heart—naïvely not realising that for him sex was simply
a pleasurable experience that meant nothing to him. Now
she was older and wiser, and she understood that desire
and love were not inextricably entwined.

She would not be so careless with her heart again, she
thought as she stared at her smudged reflection in the
steamed-up mirror. In fact, since her marriage to Simon
had proved to be such a mistake, she had lost all confidence
in her judgement and wondered if she would ever fall in
love again.

But she was not an over-awed eighteen-year-old with a
head full of unrealistic expectations, she reminded herself.
She knew Lanzo had desired her tonight, and she could
not deny her fierce attraction to him. She could not allow
her experiences with Simon to ruin the rest of her life, and
perhaps a passionate fling with a drop-dead sexy playboy
was just what she needed to restore her self-confidence
after her divorce? she mused.

But much later that night, when sleep still eluded her,
she acknowledged that only a fool played with fire and did
not expect to get burned.

CHAPTER THREE

THE *Queen of the East* was a sixty-metre-long luxury yacht owned by a wealthy Arab sheikh, and was currently moored in St Peter Port off the island of Guernsey. The yacht was certainly impressive, Lanzo thought as he steered his powerboat alongside, shrugged out of his waterproof jacket and prepared to climb aboard.

'I'm glad you could make it, my friend,' Sheikh Rashid bin Zayad Hussain greeted him. 'Your business call was successful, I hope?'

'Yes, thank you. But I apologise once again for my lateness,' Lanzo murmured, accepting a glass of champagne from a waiter and glancing around at the other guests who were milling about the yacht's breathtakingly opulent salon. 'The refit is superb, Rashid.'

'I admit I am impressed with the quality of workmanship and attention to detail by Nautica World. The company is small, but Richard Melton has certainly delivered. That is him over there.' The Sheikh dipped his head slightly. 'A pleasant fellow—married with two small children, I believe. He has built his company up from nothing, which is no mean feat in these economic times.'

Lanzo followed the Sheikh's gaze and stiffened with shock. He had been unable to dismiss Gina from his mind for the past twenty-four hours, which had made a mockery of his decision not to contact her again. He desired her, but it was more than that. He was intrigued by her, and curious to discover why she was so different from the girl he had once known.

'Is the woman with Melton his wife?' he demanded tersely.

'The beautiful brunette in the white dress?' Sheikh Hussain looked over at the Englishman, whose hand was resting lightly on his female companion's slender waist. 'No. He simply introduced her as a friend when they came on board. I have met Mrs Melton once, and I understand that she is expecting another child.' To the Sheikh's mind there was only one explanation as to the identity of the mystery woman. 'It would seem that Richard Melton's good taste extends to his choice of mistress,' he murmured.

Lanzo's jaw hardened as he stared at Gina and her male companion. Last night he had puzzled over why she had seemed so wary of him, and had felt concerned that she had been hurt by an event or a person in her past. But now, as he noted her designer dress and the exquisite pearl necklace around her throat, he was sure he had imagined the air of mystery about her, and cynically wondered if she rejected him in favour of a married lover.

'So, what do you think of the yacht?'

Gina glanced at her brother-in-law and grimaced. 'It's stunning, but a bit over the top for my liking,' she replied honestly. 'There's a lot of gold. Do you know that even the taps in the bathroom are gold-plated? Well, of course you know—your company was responsible for the refit. I suppose the important thing is that Sheikh Hussain likes it.'

Richard grinned. 'He loves it—which is why he's throwing a party to show it off. Even better, several of his friends here tonight also own yachts and are interested in having them refitted, which is good news for Nautica World.' He paused. 'Thanks for accompanying me tonight, Gina. The party is a fantastic opportunity to drum up new business. Usually Sarah comes with me, but she's finding the last few weeks of this pregnancy exhausting, and I know she was grateful you agreed to take her place.'

'I'm happy to help,' Gina said easily. Her smile faded as she thought of her stepsister. 'Sarah does seem a bit fed up—but I suppose three pregnancies in four years is a lot to cope with.'

'To be perfectly honest, this last baby was a bit of a mistake,' Richard admitted ruefully. 'I only have to look at Sarah and she falls pregnant,' he joked.

Lucky Sarah, Gina thought wistfully. Her stepsister had no idea what it was like to be unable to conceive, to have your hopes dashed every month, and to feel a pang of longing every time you saw a newborn baby.

She knew her family would have been surprised to learn that she and Simon had tried for over a year to have a child. 'Oh, Gina is a career woman,' they'd explained, whenever the question of babies was mentioned by other relatives. She had never spoken about her infertility; she felt enough of a failure as it was, without her family's well meaning sympathy. And so now she smiled at her brother-in-law and bit back the comment that she would give anything to be happily married with two adorable children and a third on the way.

Richard glanced across the salon. 'You see that man over there?' he murmured. 'He's one of Sheikh Hussain's cousins, and he owns a forty-foot motor cruiser. I think I'll go and have a chat with him.'

Gina laughed. 'I hope you can convince him that he needs Nautica World's services.' She was very fond of her brother-in-law. Richard worked hard, and certainly deserved to be successful.

'You look stunning tonight, *cara*.'

The familiar, sexy drawl caused Gina to spin round, and her heart missed a beat when her eyes clashed with Lanzo's glinting green gaze. Once again his appearance had taken her by surprise, and she had no time to disguise her reaction to him, colour flaring in her cheeks as she acknowledged how incredibly handsome he looked in a black dinner jacket and a snowy white shirt that contrasted with his darkly tanned skin.

'If I'm not mistaken, your dress is a couture creation. Business must be booming if your boyfriend can afford to buy you pearls and designer clothes, as well as supporting his children and a pregnant wife,' he drawled.

Gina stared at him, puzzled by his words and the flare of contempt in his eyes. 'I don't have a boyfriend—married or otherwise,' she told him shortly.

'You're saying that you are not Richard Melton's mistress?'

Shock rendered her speechless for twenty seconds. '*No!* I mean, *yes*. That's exactly what I'm saying.' Twin spots of angry colour flared on Gina's cheeks. 'Of course I'm not Richard's *mistress*.' Her fingers strayed unwittingly to the rope of perfect white pearls around her neck. 'Why on earth would you think that?'

Lanzo's eyes narrowed. 'Sheikh Hussain has met Melton's wife. Why else would he parade you on his arm if you are not lovers?'

'He's my brother-in-law,' she explained angrily. 'Richard is married to my stepsister. Sarah is expecting a baby in a few weeks, and she was too tired to attend the party tonight, so I came with Richard instead.'

She thought of all the newspaper stories she had read

over the years about Lanzo's numerous affairs with glamorous mistresses. The Sheikh was no better. Richard had told her he had a wife in Dubai, but he was obviously having an affair with the voluptuous redhead who was hanging on his arm tonight.

She gave a harsh laugh. 'You and your Sheikh friend might be notorious womanisers, but don't judge everyone by your low standards. Richard is devoted to Sarah and the boys, and I would *never*—' She broke off, suddenly aware that her raised voice was drawing attention from other guests. 'I would never have a relationship with a married man. My necklace was left to me by my grandmother, if you must know,' she said coldly, dismayed to feel her heart-rate quicken when Lanzo ran his fingertip lightly over the pearls and then, by accident or design, traced the line of her collarbone.

'The pearls were a wedding present to Nonna Ginevra from my grandfather, and I'll always treasure them.' Her grandparents had been happily married for sixty years before they had died within a few months of each other. Gina regarded the necklace as a symbol of hope that marriages could last, even though hers had ended after two years. She glared at Lanzo. 'Excuse me, I need some fresh air,' she snapped, and spun round to walk away from him.

She had only taken two steps when a voice called her name.

'Gina—just the person I wanted to see. You'll be pleased to know that I've found tenants who want to rent your flat.'

Gina smiled faintly at Geoffrey Robins, who owned an estate agency in Poole. 'That *is* good news,' she agreed.

'They want to move in at the end of the month, if that suits you. And the rent they are prepared to pay will cover your mortgage repayments. Did you say you were going to move back to your father's place until you find another job?' Geoffrey asked her. 'Only I heard on the grapevine that Peter is putting the farm on the market following his heart attack.'

She nodded. 'Yes, Dad *is* selling the farm. But Sarah and Hazel have both said that I can stay with them, and hopefully I'll find a job soon.' Both her stepsisters had growing families and small houses. Moving in with one or other of them was not going to be ideal, but Gina knew that her only hope of keeping her flat was to rent it out for a few months.

'Well, I'll catch up with you next week and let you know a few more details,' Geoffrey said. His eyes lit up when he saw a waiter approach them. 'Ah, I think I'll have another glass of that excellent Burgundy.' He reached out his hand to take a glass of wine, but as he did so the waiter stumbled, the glasses on the tray shot forward, and Gina gave a cry as red wine cascaded down the front of her dress.

'Scusi! Mi dispiace tanto, signora!' The horrified waiter apologised profusely in his native Italian. The yacht's crew were of a variety of nationalities, and this waiter was young and very good-looking—another heartbreaker in the making, Gina thought wryly.

'E'bene. Non si preoccupy.' It's fine. Don't worry, she assured him calmly.

'Apparently the best way to remove a red wine stain is to cover it in white wine,' Geoffrey advised, handing her a small white handkerchief which was of no use at all.

'I'm quite wet enough, thanks,' Gina said dryly, supremely conscious of the interested glances she was receiving from the other guests.

She *was* annoyed that her dress was probably ruined. Her days of being able to afford expensive clothes, which had been a requirement of her job at Meyers, were over, and she would not be able to replace the dress. But far worse was the knowledge that she was the centre of attention. She frantically scanned the salon for Richard, her heart sinking when she saw that he was still deep in conversation with a potential client.

'Come with me,' a deep, gravelly voice commanded, and before she could think of arguing Lanzo had slipped his hand beneath her elbow and steered her swiftly through the throng of guests out onto the deck.

'I don't believe it,' she muttered as she dabbed ineffectively at the spreading wine stain with the handkerchief. 'Dinner is going to be served in a few minutes. I wonder if the Sheikh has anything I could change into?'

'I doubt it. Rashid probably keeps a selection of skimpy negligees for his mistresses, but you might not feel comfortable wearing one to dinner.'

'You're right. I wouldn't,' Gina muttered, infuriated by the amused gleam in Lanzo's eyes.

'There's only one thing to do. I'll take you home.'

She glanced pointedly at the sea stretching far into the distance. The English coastline was not even visible. 'What a brilliant suggestion,' she said sarcastically. 'The only snag is that I can't swim that far.'

'You don't have to, *cara*. My boat is moored alongside the yacht.'

Frowning, Gina followed Lanzo to the stern of the yacht and stared down at his powerboat. 'I'm not sure…' she said doubtfully.

'Come on.' He was already climbing down the ladder which hung over the side of the yacht, and glanced up at her impatiently. 'Climb down. Don't worry. I'll catch you if you fall.'

Gina hesitated, deeply reluctant to go with Lanzo. Her

heart had leapt the instant she had seen him tonight, and she was irritated that she seemed incapable of controlling her reaction to him. But the red wine had soaked through her dress, and she felt sticky and urgently in need of a shower.

'All right,' she said slowly. 'But you won't go too fast, will you?'

'Of course not,' he assured her smoothly.

It was no easy feat to climb down the ladder in heels and a long skirt, and she gasped when strong hands settled around her waist and Lanzo lowered her into his boat.

'There's not a lot of room.' He stated the obvious as he helped her slide into one of the two front seats, before easing himself behind the wheel. 'Powerboats are designed for speed rather than comfort. Here—slip this around your shoulders,' he told her as he shrugged out of his dinner jacket and handed it to her. 'It might help shield you from the spray.'

His voice was drowned out by the throaty throb of the engine, and as the boat shot forward Gina gripped the edge of her seat and closed her eyes. 'Remember you promised not to go too fast,' she yelled, but her words were whipped away on the wind.

'Didn't you find that exhilarating?' Lanzo demanded, a hair-raising half-hour later, as he cut the throttle and steered the boat alongside a private jetty in Poole Harbour.

Gina unclenched her fingers from the edge of her seat and put a shaky hand up to push the hair out of her eyes. They had sped across the sea so fast that the wind had whipped the clip from her chignon, and now her hair fell in a tangled mass down her back. 'That's not quite how I would describe it,' she said curtly. 'I was terrified.'

'You had no reason to be.' He frowned when he saw how

pale she was. 'I know what I'm doing. You were perfectly safe with me.'

She did not doubt his ability to handle the powerboat, but she did not feel safe with Lanzo even on dry land, Gina admitted to herself. She did not fear that he would hurt her, as Simon had done. Her wariness stemmed from the feelings he evoked in her—the hot, flustered feeling of sexual desire that she had not felt for a very long time.

She looked up at the row of huge houses set back from the jetty and stiffened. 'Why have we come to Sandbanks?' she asked sharply. 'I thought you were going to take me home.'

'I have brought you to my home. My housekeeper will know how to clean that wine stain.' Lanzo had jumped onto the jetty and, ignoring her mutinous expression, swung her into his arms and set her down beside him. 'I want to talk to you.'

'About what?' she demanded suspiciously.

'I have a proposition that I am confident will suit both of us. Come up to the house and we can discuss it,' he ordered, and strode along the jetty, leaving Gina with no option but to trail after him.

Twenty minutes later she emerged from the marble-tiled bathroom Lanzo had shown her to after he had ushered her into his house, feeling considerably cleaner after a shower. She had blasted her hair with a hairdryer and donned a white towelling robe, and now she stepped hesitantly into the main hall, wondering what to do.

'Feeling better?' Lanzo strolled through one of the doors leading off the hall. 'Daphne has prepared us something to eat. Come on through.'

He had discarded his bow tie and unfastened the top few buttons of his shirt to reveal several inches of bronzed skin overlaid with whorls of dark chest hair. Gina's stomach lurched and she took a steadying breath. 'Who is Daphne?'

'My housekeeper, cook and general all-round saint. Daphne travels with me to my various houses around the world, and is the only woman I can't live without,' he told her, his smile revealing his perfect white teeth.

It transpired that Daphne was a tiny, dark-haired woman with a lined brown face and brilliant black eyes. Why on earth did she feel so pleased that Lanzo's housekeeper was not a gorgeous, leggy blonde? Gina asked herself irritably as she followed him into a huge open-plan lounge, with floor-to-ceiling windows that looked out over the sea.

'What an incredible view,' she murmured, distracted from her acute awareness of him for a few moments. 'My flat overlooks the harbour, but the view is nothing as spectacular as this.'

Sliding glass doors opened onto a decked area where a table was laid with a selection of colourful salad dishes and crusty rolls. Of course—they had missed dinner aboard the yacht, Gina remembered, discovering suddenly that she was hungry.

'I didn't know that you speak Italian,' Lanzo commented when they had sat down and he'd indicated that she should help herself to food.

'My grandmother taught me. She moved to England when she married my grandfather, but she missed Italy and loved to speak her own language.'

'Whereabouts in Italy did she come from?'

'Rome.' Gina heaped crispy lettuce leaves onto her plate, and topped them with a slice of round, creamy white mozzarella cheese. 'I've been there several times for work, but never had time to explore the city. One day I plan to go back and look for the house where Nonna used to live.'

'Di Cosimo Holdings' head offices are in Rome.' Lanzo

filled two glasses with wine and handed her one. 'To old friendships and new beginnings,' he murmured, touching his glass to hers.

'Oh…yes…' Gina hesitated fractionally. 'To old friendships.' She wasn't convinced about new beginnings, and to avoid his speculative gaze she took a sip of deliciously cool Chardonnay.

'Come and work for me and I promise I'll give you a guided tour of the city. I know Rome well, and I'm sure I'll be able to find your grandmother's house.'

Her eyes flew to his face. She had been so absorbed in her intense awareness of him last night that she had forgotten his offer for her to work for him as a temporary PA. Now she hurriedly shook her head. 'No—I don't think so.'

'Why are you so quick to dismiss the idea?' Lanzo sat back and studied her broodingly. 'And why do you need to rent out your flat?'

'Were you eavesdropping on my conversation with Geoffrey?' Gina began hotly.

'I was standing close by and couldn't help but overhear.'

She was tempted to tell him to mind his own business, but after a moment she shrugged and put down her fork, her appetite fading as it always did when she remembered her financial worries.

'When I moved back to Poole I took out a big mortgage to buy my flat,' she admitted. 'It wasn't a problem at the time, because I was earning a good salary at Hartman Homes, but since I lost my job I've fallen behind with the repayments.'

'I'm prepared to offer you a six-month contract and pay you a generous salary—higher than you were earning at Meyers.'

Gina's brows lifted. 'That's a rather rash statement when you don't *know* what I earned at Meyers.'

'I have a fair idea. A good PA is like gold-dust, and I expect to pay good money to ensure the best staff.'

'How do you know I'm good at my job?'

He shrugged. 'I checked your references. Did you think I would offer you the vital role of my personal assistant without first making sure you could handle the responsibility?' he queried coolly when she opened her mouth to tell him he had a nerve. 'I am a businessman, *cara*, and I never allow emotions to dictate my decisions.

'I spoke to your previous boss, Frank Wallis, and he assured me that you were the most dedicated and efficient PA he'd ever had—with an almost obsessive attention to detail,' Lanzo added, looking amused. 'Apparently you had a complicated system of colour-coded notes.'

Gina flushed. 'I like to be organised,' she defended herself. Maybe she *was* a bit obsessive, but she wasn't a control freak as Simon had accused her of being. She simply liked things to run like clockwork.

'I have no problem with you being organised,' Lanzo assured her. 'In fact it is a necessity. I work long hours and travel extensively. I will expect you to accompany me on business trips and also to act as my hostess occasionally when I hold social functions.'

He was going way too fast, Gina thought frantically, panic flaring inside her that he seemed to think her agreement was a given. '*If* I accept the job,' she muttered.

'Why wouldn't you?' he demanded.

There were so many reasons, but the main one was her strong attraction to Lanzo—an attraction that she had decided during a sleepless night that she dared not take any further. He had broken her heart once, and she was not prepared to risk her peace of mind by becoming involved with him again.

But it would only be for six months, a voice in her head pointed out. His job offer was a fantastic opportunity for her to sort out her finances and ensure that she kept her flat that she loved. If she went to Italy to work for Lanzo she would not have to impose herself on her stepsisters while she rented the flat out, and the six months' rent paid by the tenants would cover the mortgage repayments. On top of that she would have six months of earning a high salary that she could put away to cover the mortgage when she returned to Poole and looked for another job.

But move to Rome, work closely with Lanzo every day, and travel to business meetings around the world with him? She chewed on her bottom lip, torn between the temptation of solving her financial problems that were growing worse with every day that she failed to find a job in Poole and fear of what she could be letting herself in for if she agreed.

What would she do if he tried to kiss her again, as he had almost done last night? She swallowed as she met his gaze and saw the banked-down flames of desire smouldering in his striking green eyes. A little tremor ran through her at the knowledge that he was attracted to her. Would it be such a disaster if she responded to him? her mind queried.

Her breath hitched in her throat as his eyes strayed down to the slopes of her breasts, visible where the edges of her robe had parted slightly. Time seemed to be suspended, and she was acutely conscious that her white dress, which was now being cleaned by Lanzo's housekeeper, had not required her to wear a bra. Her breasts felt swollen and heavy, and into her mind came the stark image of Lanzo pushing the robe over her shoulders and lowering his head to take one nipple and then its twin in his mouth.

'You would be a fool to turn me down, Gina.' His voice

jerked her back to reality and she tore her gaze from him, hot colour storming into her cheeks as she prayed he had not guessed her shocking thoughts. 'You need this job, and I need to appoint a temporary PA as soon as possible. I have excellent contacts, and when Luisa returns to work after her maternity leave I will recommend you to other company directors who may be looking for staff.'

It was an offer no sensible person could refuse. A golden chance to keep her flat, which was more than just a home but also a place where she felt safe and secure after two years of living on the edge of her nerves with Simon. She had hoped that buying the flat would be the start of a new chapter in her life—a mark of her independence now that she had escaped her violent marriage. She had vowed to take any job she could find to meet the mortgage repayments, she reminded herself. She was twenty-eight, no longer a naïve girl, and she was more than capable of dealing with her inconvenient attraction to Lanzo.

'All right,' she said quickly, before she could change her mind. 'I accept your offer.'

Lanzo was careful to hide the feeling of satisfaction that surged through him. He had realised when he had seen Gina on the yacht earlier tonight that his desire for her was too strong for him to be able to dismiss it. He wanted her, and his instincts told him that she was not as immune to him as she would like him to think. But he sensed her wariness, although he did not understand the reason for it, and knew that he would have to be patient and win her trust before he could persuade her into his bed.

'Good,' he said briskly. 'I'll pick you up from your flat at nine tomorrow morning, and my private jet will collect us from Bournemouth airport and take us to Rome. Luisa will come into the office for a couple of hours to run through everything with you.'

Gina gave him a startled look, doubts already forming thick and fast in her head. 'I'll need a few days to get myself organised. For a start I'll have to find somewhere to stay in Rome.'

'You can stay at my apartment. It will be ideal,' he insisted when she opened her mouth to object. 'I often work late in the evenings, and it will be useful to have you on hand. I hope you weren't thinking that this was going to be a nine-to-five job?' Lanzo said abruptly, noticing her doubtful expression. 'For the money I'll be paying you I will expect your full and exclusive attention twenty-four-seven.'

'Presumably my nights will be my own?' she replied coolly, stung by his tone. She was well aware that the job of PA to the head of a global company meant working extended hours, including evenings and weekends when required, but she would need to sleep!

Lanzo leaned back in his chair and surveyed her with a wicked gleam in his eyes. 'Certainly—if you want them to be, *cara*,' he murmured softly. Was she aware of the hungry glances she had been darting at him across the table? he wondered. Or the way the pulse at the base of her throat was jerking frantically beneath her skin?

Under ordinary circumstances he would not consider mixing his work with his personal life. Office relationships always created problems, which was why he never had affairs with his staff. But the current circumstances were not ordinary.

It had come as a bolt from the blue when his PA of the last five years had suddenly announced that she was getting married, and then a few months later revealed that she was pregnant. Of course he was pleased for Luisa—although somewhat surprised, because she had never given any indication that she wanted to settle down to a life of domestic bliss. But he resented the disruption her pregnancy had caused to his life. Two junior secretaries had jointly taken over organising his diary, but he missed Luisa's calm efficiency that had ensured his office ran as smoothly as a well-oiled machine.

His conversation with Gina's retired boss from Meyers had convinced him that she was ideally suited to fill the position of his temporary PA. But, more than that, it was a chance for him to get to know her again. She had lingered in his mind for a long time after he had returned to Italy ten years ago. They had been friends as well as lovers, and now it was perfectly natural for him be intrigued by her, he assured himself.

It went without saying that any relationship he might have with her would not involve his emotions. After the fire fifteen years ago had taken everyone he had loved he had felt frozen inside. His heart was as cold and hard as a lump of ice, and he was not sure than anything would ever make it thaw.

CHAPTER FOUR

'What was the name of that little country pub in the New Forest that we used to go to?' Lanzo queried. 'Do you remember it? We went there several times.'

Of course she remembered, Gina thought silently. She remembered every place she had visited with Lanzo ten years ago. 'It was the Hare and Hounds, famous for its steak and ale pies,' she told him. 'You took me there for lunch on my days off from the restaurant.'

'Mmm—and afterwards we went walking in the forest.'

They had walked deep among the trees and made love in a little clearing, where the sun had filtered through the leafy canopy above and dappled their bodies. Gina inhaled sharply. 'Yes, we went on some lovely walks,' she murmured, pretending to clear her throat to disguise the huskiness of her voice. 'The New Forest is very pretty.'

'We made love in a little dell, hidden among the trees.' Lanzo stretched his long legs out in front of him and turned his head towards Gina, his mouth curving into a sensual smile when she blushed. 'Do you remember, *cara*?'

'Vaguely.' She affected an uninterested shrug. 'It was a long time ago.' She stared out of the window of Lanzo's private jet at the endless expanse of brilliant blue sky, and tried to ignore her fierce awareness of him. It wasn't easy when he was sitting next to her, his body half turned to hers so that her eyes were drawn to his face, and inevitably, to the sensual curve of his mouth.

She had only spent three hours in his company since he had picked her up from her flat that morning, but she was already losing the battle to remain immune to his charisma, she thought dismally. When he had taken the seat next to her on the plane she had assumed he would open his laptop and catch up on some work, but instead he had spent the entire flight chatting to her and reminiscing about the past.

To be honest she was surprised at how much he remembered of their affair. They had only been lovers for a matter of weeks, yet Lanzo recalled the places they had visited together, as well as those passionate sex sessions in the forest, which were branded indelibly in her memory but which she'd thought he had forgotten.

'How much longer until we land?' she asked him briskly. Perhaps once they were at the Di Cosimo offices in Rome she would be able to slip into the role of efficient PA, and her heart would stop leaping every time he smiled at her?

'We won't be long now. The pilot has just indicated that we should fasten our seatbelts,' he told her, his eyes glinting with amusement when she gave an audible sigh of relief.

Rome in late June was stiflingly hot; the temperature displayed on the information board at Fiumcino Airport showed thirty-two degrees Celsius, and Gina was glad to slide into the cool interior of Lanzo's waiting limousine.

'We'll go straight to the office,' he told her as the car moved smoothly into the stream of traffic heading in the direction of the city centre. 'Luisa is going to be there to hand over to you. This afternoon I'm holding a board meeting and I'll require you to take the minutes.'

As he spoke his phone bleeped, and he began to scroll

through his messages while simultaneously checking emails on his laptop. The powerboat racer playboy had been replaced by the powerful billionaire businessman, Gina mused. Dressed in a beautifully tailored dark grey suit, blue silk shirt, and toning tie, he was achingly sexy. She sighed and tore her eyes from him. She had barely slept last night, plagued by doubts over her decision to work for him. She had no qualms about her ability to cope with the demands of the job of his PA, but she was less confident about her ability to deal with the devastating affect he had on her peace of mind.

'I'm afraid my Italian might be a bit rusty,' she said worriedly. 'I spent six months working for an Italian company in Milan, but that was before…' She had been about to say *before I got married*, but she had no desire to talk about Simon—her marriage had been a bleak period of her life she preferred to forget. 'That was a few years ago,' she said instead. 'You'll have to ask your board members to be patient with me.'

'Don't worry about it. Di Cosimo Holdings is a global company and the board members are not all Italian. Meetings are usually conducted in English,' Lanzo explained.

Privately, he did not think the members of the board would be overly concerned with Gina's language skills and were far more likely to focus their attention on her curvaceous figure. Presumably her aim had been to look smart and efficient, in a pale grey suit teamed with a lilac-coloured blouse, but the pencil skirt moulded her derrière so that it swayed delightfully when she walked, and the cut of her jacket emphasised her slender waist and her full breasts. Long, slim legs sheathed in sheer hose, and high-heeled black stilettos completed her outfit, and the whole effect was one of understated elegance that could not hide the fact that Gina was a sexy and desirable woman.

Lanzo took a sharp breath. He had spent the entire flight fantasising about leading Gina into the bedroom at the rear of the plane and unbuttoning that prim blouse. He could see the faint outline of her lacy bra beneath it, and in the fantasy he had peeled the straps over her shoulders so that her ample breasts spilled into his hands. Patience was all very well, but his determination to take things slowly was already wearing thin, and he was wondering how quickly he could persuade her to lower her barriers. One thing was certain: he would have to subtly let it be known to his board members that his temporary PA was off-limits to anyone but him, he decided.

'I'm sure it won't take you long to settle in,' he murmured. 'Do you like pizza?'

'I love it—unfortunately.' Gina grimaced. 'I'm afraid my hips don't need any encouragement to expand.'

'You look in perfect proportion to me.' Lanzo subjected her to a leisurely inspection that made her feel hot and flustered. 'I agree you're not a bag of bones, in the way so many women seem to think is attractive, but you won't find any complaints here in Italy, *cara*. Italian men like their women to be curvaceous. At least...' He paused and trapped her gaze with his mesmeric green eyes. 'At least this Italian male does.'

He was blatantly flirting with her, Gina realised, irritated by her body's instinctive reaction to him. She wanted to tell him to back off—that the hungry gleam in his eyes was totally inappropriate when she was one of his employees.

What chance did she stand of resisting him when he turned on his full mega-watt charm? she thought despairingly. But Lanzo could not help flirting with women—all women. It was as natural to him as breathing, and it didn't mean anything. The best way to deal with it was to ignore it, she told herself firmly.

'Why did you want to know if I like pizza?' she said lightly. 'Were you going to recommend a good restaurant?'

'Agnelli's—it's a little place tucked away down a side-street, off the main tourist trail, and it serves the best pizza in Rome. I thought we could eat there tonight.'

'Please don't feel you have to entertain me,' Gina said quickly. 'I'm sure you have a busy social life, and I'm quite happy to do my own thing.'

His smile made her heart flip. 'But we are old friends, Gina,' he said softly. 'I want to spend time with you.'

Oh, hell! Did he have any idea how emotive she found the expression *old friends*? How it tugged on her heart and sent her mind spinning back to those few weeks many years ago when she had been so insanely happy? Perhaps the happiest she had ever been in her life, a little voice inside her head whispered.

The atmosphere inside the car suddenly seemed taut with tension. The rumble of traffic outside faded, and Gina was painfully conscious of the ragged sound of her breathing. Coming to Italy with him had been a mistake, she thought frantically. Yet she could not deny that she felt more alive than she had felt for a long, long time.

She could not tear her eyes from his mouth, and memories filled her mind of him kissing her with hungry passion all those years ago. His reminiscing over their affair had made her remember how gentle he had been with her the first time he had made love to her. Her ex-husband had rarely been tender, and had taken his own pleasure with selfish disregard for hers. Her unsatisfying sex life had been one of the first disappointments of her marriage, Gina thought ruefully. She had not known in those early days how much worse her relationship with Simon would become.

Every instinct she possessed told her that Lanzo was nothing like Simon and that he would never hurt her—not physically, at any rate. It was the threat he posed to her emotional security that worried her. When his mouth curved into a slow smile everything flew from her mind but her yearning for him to brush his lips over hers and then deepen the kiss until he obliterated all her fears.

She caught her breath when he leaned towards her, but then he stilled and she felt sick inside, knowing that he had noticed her scar. She had been in such a rush that morning, at the last minute frantically packing belongings she had thought she would need in Italy, and she had not taken as much care as usual to conceal her scar with make-up. She tried to jerk away from him, but he slid his hand beneath her chin and gently forced her to look at him.

'That must have been a nasty wound,' he said quietly. 'What happened?'

'I had an accident a year or so ago,' she muttered, pulling her hair around her face to cover the scar. She swallowed. 'It's horrible. It makes me feel so ugly.'

Lanzo gave her a puzzled look. 'What kind of accident—a car crash?' He hazarded a guess. The scar was a long thin line that ran down her face, beneath her ear and a little way down her neck. He could only think that she had been cut—perhaps by glass when a windscreen had shattered.

Gina shook her head. 'It's not important.' The matter of how she had gained her scar was absolutely off-limits. She never spoke of it to anyone—not even her family.

Lanzo hesitated, and then said matter-of-factly, 'It hardly shows, and it certainly does not make you look ugly, *cara*. Nothing could diminish your beauty.'

His smile deepened as she gave him a startled glance.

When she blushed she reminded him of the shy waitress who had had a crush on him years ago, who had responded to him with such sweet passion when he had kissed her. He wondered what she would do if he kissed her now. Probably she would jerk away from him like a frightened doe, as she had done when he had walked her home from the Di Cosimo restaurant in Poole. He would like to meet whoever was responsible for causing the fearful look in her eyes, Lanzo thought grimly.

The car came to a halt and Gina released a shaky breath as the chauffeur opened the door for her to step out onto the pavement. Minutes later she followed Lanzo through the tinted glass doors of Di Cosimo Holdings. She was acutely conscious of him as they silently rode the lift up to the top floor, and her hand strayed unwittingly to the long scar hidden beneath her hair as she remembered how he had told her she was beautiful *after* he had seen the unsightly bluish line.

Perhaps her overwhelming awareness of Lanzo was not so surprising. He had been her first lover, and sex with him had been utterly fulfilling. Was it so wrong to want to experience the pleasure of his lovemaking again? To revel in his hard, muscular body skilfully possessing hers, and to make love to him in return—two people meeting as equals and taking each other to the heights of sexual ecstasy?

The lift halted, and as the door slid open she forced her turbulent thoughts to the back of her mind. Now was not an appropriate time to be imagining Lanzo's naked aroused body. *Was* there an appropriate time? she wondered wildly. She had come to Italy to work for him, and she was determined to fulfil the role of his PA with quiet professionalism, she reminded herself firmly.

'Welcome to Di Cosimo Holdings. Come and meet my team,' Lanzo said smoothly. His eyes lingered speculatively on her flushed face, but, calling on all her acting skills, Gina gave him a cool smile and followed him into his office.

Despite being heavily pregnant, Luisa Bartolli was still incredibly elegant, as so many continental women were, Gina thought to herself. Lanzo's PA was also friendly and welcoming, and clearly relieved to meet her temporary replacement.

'Lanzo wasn't impressed when I told him I would be having a few months off to have a baby,' Luisa confided as she gave Gina a tour of the offices. 'I've been his PA for over five years, and I know how much he dislikes any disruption to his routine. But it can't be helped.' She shrugged. 'Until I met my husband I had no plans to marry or have children. But Marco was keen to have a family, and I'm so excited about the baby. I'm thirty-six, and I know I'm lucky to have conceived the first month we tried. I haven't dared mention it to Lanzo yet, but I'm already thinking that I don't want to come back to work full-time and put the baby in day care.' Luisa added. She glanced at Gina. 'I'm sure that with your experience as a PA you'll get on fine working for him. Perhaps you would consider job-sharing with me after my maternity leave is over?'

'I don't think so,' Gina replied hastily. She already had doubts about the wisdom of agreeing to spend the next six months working for Lanzo. She certainly did not plan to extend her time with him. 'I have a flat back in England, and I need to work full-time to pay my mortgage.' She smiled at Luisa. 'Everything seems straightforward, but thanks for saying that I can ring you if I have any problems.' She stared wistfully at Luisa's bump. 'When is the baby due?'

'Not for another six weeks.' Luisa grimaced. 'I feel fine,

but the doctor has told me to rest, and Marco won't allow me to do *anything*. He only allowed me to come into the office today after I promised to spend the rest of the day with my feet up.'

'Your husband is obviously determined to take good care of you,' Gina murmured, stifling a little stab of envy. Her marriage to Simon had been in trouble barely months after the wedding. The charming man who had wined and dined her for six months before he had whisked her away for a romantic weekend in Paris and proposed at the top of the Eiffel Tower had changed overnight, it had seemed, into a possessive husband of unpredictable moods who had been jealous of her friendships and subjected her to verbal abuse when he was drunk.

It was probably a good thing that she had failed to fall pregnant, Gina conceded. Simon's increasing dependence on alcohol meant that he would not have been a good father. She had tried to help him, but it was impossible to help someone who refused to recognise he had a problem, and in the end, for the sake of her sanity and increasingly her physical safety, she had left him.

After Luisa had left, Gina got straight down to business and quickly became absorbed in the pile of paperwork on her desk. It felt good to be back at work. She was not naturally idle, and had hated her enforced weeks of inactivity after she had lost her job in Poole.

She took the minutes of the board meeting, relieved to find that the board members were indeed a mixture of nationalities and everyone spoke English, so her fluency in Italian was not put to the test on her first day. Lanzo had further meetings booked for the rest of the day, but at five he called her into his office and told her that he had arranged for his driver to take her back to his apartment.

'You've done enough for today,' he said, when she

protested that she was happy to stay on until he had finished. 'Go and relax for a couple of hours and I'll meet you at home later.'

Trying not to dwell on the fact that she would be sharing his home for the next few months, she arrived at his penthouse apartment, close to the famous Spanish Steps, and was greeted by Daphne.

'I have unpacked for you,' the housekeeper explained as she led the way to the guest bedroom which, like all the other rooms in the apartment, was decorated in neutral colours. It was not a very homely home—more like a five-star hotel, Gina mused as she glanced around at the ultra-modern décor. Her thoughts must have shown on her face, because Daphne explained, 'Lanzo's real home is his villa on the Amalfi Coast. He only stays here when he needs to be at the head office. Would you like a cup of English tea? He told me to buy it especially for you, because he remembered that you always used to drink it.'

Don't read too much into it, Gina told herself firmly. She smiled at the housekeeper. 'Tea would be lovely, thank you.'

When Daphne had gone she made a quick inspection of her room and the *en suite* bathroom, and then stripped out of her work clothes and stepped into the shower. Ten minutes later she pulled on a cool white cotton sundress, collected her tea from the kitchen, and wandered out onto the roof terrace—a leafy oasis of potted plants with spectacular views across Rome.

She would find her grandmother's house while she was here, Gina decided. It was exciting to be in the historical city, and she was looking forward to playing tourist and visiting the ancient landmarks. For the first time in months she felt her spirits lift—and if her excitement stemmed mainly from the fact that she would be spending the next few months with Lanzo, then so be it, she thought defensively. She was a grown woman and she could look after herself.

An hour later she stirred at the sound of her name, and opened her eyes to find Lanzo standing beside the lounger where she had fallen asleep.

'You should have sat beneath the parasol,' he told her, hunkering down beside her and running his fingers lightly up her arm. 'At this time of the year the sun is still strong until late in the evening, and your fair skin could easily burn.'

'I didn't mean to go to sleep,' she mumbled, jerking upright and pushing her hair back from her hot face. 'I was going to finish typing up the notes from the board meeting.' She stared at him dazedly, her brain still fogged with sleep, and her heart rate quickened when she saw that he had changed into faded jeans and a tight fitting black tee shirt that moulded his broad chest. His hair was still damp from where he had showered, and his hypnotic green eyes gleamed with a hunger he made no effort to disguise. 'When did you get back?' she mumbled, unable to drag her eyes from the chiselled perfection of his handsome face.

'Ten minutes ago.' Lanzo did not add that he had been impatient for his meeting to finish so that he could come home to her. In her simple summer dress she did not look much older than she had at eighteen, he brooded, fighting the urge to tangle his fingers in her long, silky chestnut hair and tilt her head so that he could claim her mouth in a kiss that he knew would not be enough for either of them.

But the faint wariness in her blue eyes cautioned him to bide his time. Gina could not hide her desire for him, however much she tried, but something was holding her back, and he was prepared to wait until she had dealt with whatever demons were bothering her.

'Now that you're awake, are you ready to sample the finest pizza in Rome?' he asked lightly. He held out his hand and, after hesitating for a moment, she placed her fingers in his and allowed him to pull her to her feet. 'Let's go and eat, *cara*. I don't know about you, but I'm starving.'

As Lanzo had said, Agnelli's pizzeria was off the tourist track, tucked away down a narrow side-street that they had reached after a fifteen-minute walk through Rome. From the outside the peeling paint around the front window and the restaurant's air of general shabbiness was not inviting, but when they walked in they were greeted warmly by the staff. Signor Agnelli hurried out of the kitchen, the apron tied around his girth dusty with white flour, and pulled Lanzo into a bear-hug, before ushering them over to a table set in a quiet corner, which he clearly reserved for his close friends.

'Enrico and I go back a long way,' Lanzo confirmed when Gina commented that the restaurant-owner seemed to regard him as a long-lost brother. He did not add that Enrico Agnelli had been one of the first firemen to arrive at the di Cosimo home in Positano on the night of the fire, and that the fireman had almost lost his life trying to save Cristina and Lanzo's parents. The injuries he had received had meant that he had had to leave the fire service, and Lanzo had willingly given his financial backing to help Enrico move to Rome and open the pizzeria.

'That was truly the best pizza I've ever eaten,' Gina said as she finished her last mouthful and sat back in her chair with a contented sigh.

'I'll tell Enrico—he'll be pleased.'

Lanzo's smile made her heart lurch, and she took a hurried sip of her wine, but nothing could distract her from her acute awareness of him, Gina acknowledged ruefully.

He had ignored the cutlery on the table and eaten his pizza with his hands, his evident enjoyment of the food somehow innately sensual. She had been happy to follow suit, and as she'd licked a smear of tomato sauce from her finger she had glanced across the table and found him watching with an intentness that had sent heat coursing through her veins.

They wandered back to his apartment in relaxed silence, and as Gina stared up at the stars glinting in the velvet blackness of the sky she felt a curious lightness inside that she realised with a jolt of shock was sheer happiness. She hadn't thought about Simon and the miserable months when their divorce had become increasingly acrimonious all day. Instead her mind had been full of Lanzo. Sitting across the table from him in Angelli's, she had found herself imagining him *sans* his shirt and hip-hugging jeans, and had pictured the two of them naked on a bed, his bare golden skin gleaming like satin, his powerful arousal rock-hard as he lowered himself onto her...

As the lift whisked them up to the penthouse she could not bring herself to look at him, conscious that her cheeks were burning. Out of the corner of her eye she saw him lift his hand, and stiffened when he lightly touched her arm. Only then did she realise that the strap of her sundress and slipped over her shoulder, revealing a lot more of the upper slope of her breast than she deemed decent. She held her breath when he tugged the strap back into place, and his drawled, 'I'm sure you don't want to fall out of your dress, *cara*,' made her face burn even hotter.

What if, instead of pulling her dress strap up, he had drawn it lower, until he had bared her breast, then shaped it with his palm, stroked his finger over her nipple...?

Her legs felt weak as she followed him into the apartment. Get a grip, she told herself furiously. But she could not control her body's response to Lanzo. He evoked feelings inside her she had thought were dead, had awoken her sexual desires so that for the first time in almost two years she felt a hot, damp yearning between her legs.

'Would you like a drink?' he asked as he ushered her into the lounge. 'A brandy—or I can make you a cup of tea?' Lanzo's eyes narrowed speculatively on Gina's flushed face. Did she know that he could decipher every one of the thoughts that darkened her blue eyes to the colour of midnight? he brooded, hunger and frustration coiling in his gut when she quickly shook her head.

'I think I'll go straight to bed. It's been a long day.' And she was going to make a complete fool of herself if she remained with him for a second longer. 'Goodnight,' she mumbled, and shot down the hallway to her bedroom, closing the door behind her and finally releasing the breath that had been trapped in her lungs.

Things could not continue like this, Gina decided after she had changed into her nightdress, brushed her teeth and climbed into bed—only to find that sleep was impossible while she was imagining Lanzo in his room just along the hall, stripping out of his clothes and sliding into his bed. Did he still sleep naked, as he had done ten years ago? Stop it, she ordered herself, punching her pillows into a more comfortable shape for the umpteenth time.

An hour later she was still wide awake, and now she was thirsty. Knowing that she would never be able to sleep until she'd had a drink, she slid out of bed and stepped into the hall. Everywhere was in darkness, and she assumed Lanzo had gone to bed, but when she pushed open the kitchen door her heart jerked against her ribs at the sight of him leaning against the worktop, idly skimming through a newspaper. He was naked apart from the towel hitched around his waist, and droplets of water glistened on his shoulders and his damp hair, indicating that he had recently showered.

Dear heaven, he was gorgeous! He lowered the paper as Gina hovered in the doorway, his bright green eyes gleaming with amusement when she stared simply stared at him, her mouth open in a perfect *oh* of shock.

Dark eyebrows winged upwards. 'Did you want something, *cara*?'

She moistened her dry lips with her tongue, and the gleam in his eyes became intent and feral. 'I came to get a drink. I usually take a glass of water to bed with me,' she croaked.

'Lucky water,' he murmured, so softly that she wasn't sure she had heard him right. He took a glass from the cabinet, filled it from the tap, and strolled towards her. Her eyes hovered on his towel and she prayed it was securely fastened.

'Here.' He handed her the glass.

'Thank you.'

Leave now, her brain insisted urgently. But her senses were swamped by his closeness, the tantalising scent of clean, damp skin, the sensual musk of his aftershave, and something else that was irrevocably male and primitive that made every nerve-ending in her body tingle.

Green eyes meshed with sapphire-blue. 'Is there anything else you want, Gina?'

His breath whispered across her lips, and without conscious thought she parted them in silent invitation. Lanzo made a muffled sound deep in his throat as he lowered his head and grazed his mouth gently over hers.

It felt like heaven. Starbursts of colour exploded in her mind as he tasted her with delicate little sips, until he felt the little shiver of pleasure that ran through her and deepened the kiss. His lips were warm and firm, yet incredibly gentle, teasing hers apart, his tongue tracing their shape but not sliding into her mouth. Instinctively she leaned closer to him. He lifted his hand and threaded his fingers through her hair.

And then suddenly, from nowhere, Simon's image hurtled into her mind—a memory of him grabbing her hair and pulling several strands from her scalp during one of his drunken rages.

'No!' She jerked away from Lanzo so forcefully that she banged the back of her head on the doorframe. He frowned and lowered his hand. She could see the questions forming on his lips and she shook her head, silently telling him that she was not about to give an explanation for her behaviour. 'I can't.' Her voice was thick with misery. 'I'm sorry.'

She was still clutching the glass, and she spun away from him so urgently that water sloshed over the rim, soaking through her nightdress as she tore down the hall towards her room.

Lanzo watched her go, half tempted to follow her and demand to know what she was playing at. She had turned from soft and willing to tense and *frightened* in the space of a few seconds, and he wanted to know why. But he recalled the expression in her eyes—a silent plea for him to back off—and after a moment he switched off the kitchen light and padded down the hall to his own room, wondering what had happened in her past that had decimated her trust.

CHAPTER FIVE

GINA dreaded facing Lanzo the following morning, but to her relief he greeted her with a casual smile when she joined him on the terrace for breakfast, and made no reference to what had happened between them the previous night. If he was curious as to why she had reacted so badly when he had kissed her he did not allow it to show, and over coffee and the delicious herb and parmesan *frittatas* that Daphne served them he focused exclusively on work and the meetings planned for the day ahead.

A week later, Gina glanced around the quaint little courtyard tucked away down a side-street in the Campo di Fiori area of Rome, and then studied the faded photograph in her hand.

'I'm sure this is where Nonna Ginevra used to live,' she said excitedly. 'The fountain in the centre of the square is just the same, and that house over in the corner looks like the one my grandparents are standing in front of in the photo. It's amazing—this courtyard has hardly changed in over sixty years,' she murmured.

Lanzo peered over her shoulder at the photograph. 'Your grandfather is in military uniform, so I assume the picture must have been taken during the Second World War?'

Gina nodded. 'Grandad was stationed in Italy in the

war, and that's when he met Nonna. They married soon after the war ended, and she moved to the farm in Dorset with him, but she often spoke of her childhood home in Rome. It must have been hard for her to leave the place she loved, but she always said that she loved my grandfather so much that she would have lived on the moon with him if he'd asked her.'

It was hot in the enclosed courtyard, and she sat down on the stone wall surrounding the fountain, glad of the fine spray that cooled her skin.

Lanzo dropped down next to her. 'You were obviously very fond of your grandmother.'

'Yes, I was close to both my grandparents. After my mother left I spent a lot of time with them while Dad was busy on the farm. They died within a few months of each other, and although I was sad I couldn't help but be glad that they were together again,' she said softly. 'Even death didn't part them for long.'

Her grandparents' long and devoted relationship had epitomised all that marriage truly meant, she thought. Love, friendship, respect—the things she had hoped for when she had married Simon, until his drinking binges and increasingly aggressive behaviour had killed her feelings for him.

'I can't believe we've actually found Nonna's childhood home,' she said, refusing to dwell on dark memories when the sun was blazing from a cobalt blue sky. 'You seem to know every corner and backstreet of the city. Did you grow up in Rome?'

Lanzo shook his head. 'No, I was born in Positano, on the Amalfi Coast. I like Rome, and I spend a lot of time here because Di Cosimo Holdings is based here, but home is very much my villa on the clifftops, looking out over the sea.'

'I've heard that the Amalfi Coast is supposed to be one of the most beautiful places in the world,' Gina said, smiling at his enthusiasm. 'Do your family still live there?'

'I have no family. My parents died many years ago, and I was an only child.' Lanzo's tone was curiously emotionless, and his eyes were shaded by his sunglasses so that Gina could not read his expression, but something warned her that he would not welcome further questions about his family.

'I'm sorry,' she murmured. She remembered reading somewhere that he had assumed control of Di Cosimo Holdings when he had been only twenty—long before he had stayed in Poole ten years ago. Presumably he had taken over the company on the death of his father. No wonder he seemed so *detached*, she mused, trying to think of a suitable word to describe him. From the sound of it he had no one in his life he cared about, and perhaps losing his parents when he had been a young man had hardened him.

There was a proverb that stated 'no man is an island'. But Lanzo seemed to prize his independence above anything, and did not appear to need anyone. His housekeeper Daphne ran his various homes and took care of his domestic arrangements, and a ready supply of willowy blonde models satisfied his high sex-drive. She wondered if he had ever been in love, but when she darted a glance at his stern profile she dared not ask, feeling fairly certain what his answer would be.

'Now that we have found where your grandmother used to live, where would you like to visit next?' he asked after a few minutes. 'We're not far from the Piazza Navona, where the fountains are rather more spectacular than this one.' He dipped his hand in the small fountain and flicked water at her, grinning when she yelped. 'The square is world-famous, and the statues are truly worth seeing.'

'You don't have to be my tour guide all weekend,' Gina told him. 'You've already shown me so much of Rome.'

Her mind re-ran the past wonderful week. After her initial awkwardness with him that first morning she had slipped into the role of his PA with surprising ease, and a companionable relationship had quickly developed between them—although she was always conscious of the shimmering sexual chemistry simmering beneath their polite conversations.

Each evening they returned to his apartment to sample Daphne's divine cooking, and afterwards strolled around the city, admiring the exquisite architecture of the ancient landmarks and discovering secret little side-streets and courtyards where they drank Chianti beneath the striped awnings of some of the cafés.

Rome was a magical place, but in her heart Gina recognised that for her the magic was created by Lanzo as he walked close beside her, or smiled indulgently when she paused to study a pretty window box or peer into a shop window. It would be very easy to fall for him, she thought ruefully. And it was that knowledge which held her back from responding to the sultry invitation in his eyes each time she bade him goodnight every evening and went to her bedroom to sleep alone.

She was puzzled that, although he did not try to disguise the fact that he desired her, he had made no further attempt to kiss her. She supposed she should have felt reassured that he was obviously not going to pressure her in any way, but instead she lay awake every night, gripped by a restless longing as she imagined his muscular, naked body pressing down on her soft flesh, his dark head lowered to her breast.

'I've enjoyed showing you around,' he told her, his voice cutting through her erotic fantasy, so that she blushed scarlet and hastily avoided his gaze. 'We won't have another chance for a while. We'll be in St Tropez for most of next week, preparing for the launch of the new Di Cosimo restaurant, and after that I plan to spend some time in Positano.'

'I assume you'll want me to be here in Rome, to run the office while you are staying at your villa?' Gina murmured, trying not to dwell on how much she would miss him. He probably had a mistress in Positano, she thought bleakly, despising herself for the corrosive jealousy that burned like acid in her stomach.

'Of course not—I'll be working from the villa, and naturally I will require my personal assistant to be with me.'

Lanzo got to his feet and stared down at her, feeling his body stir into urgent life as his eyes were drawn to the deep valley between her breasts revealed by her low-cut vest top. After spending all week fantasising about the voluptuous curves she kept hidden beneath smart work suits and high-necked blouses, the sight of her in denim shorts and the clingy lemon yellow top at breakfast this morning had sent heat surging through his veins.

He could not remember ever wanting a woman as badly as he wanted Gina, he acknowledged, almost resenting her for the hold she seemed to have over him. He had told himself he would wait until she accepted that their mutual attraction could only have one inevitable conclusion, but he hadn't reckoned on her ability to shatter his peace of mind.

Lanzo took Gina's hand and drew her to her feet, but instead of leading her out of the courtyard he stood towering over her, so that she was faced with the choice of staring at his muscle-bound chest, and the tantalising glimpse of tanned flesh above the neckline of his shirt, or the chiselled perfection of his face.

'I want you to come to Positano with me,' he said, in

his rich-as-molten-chocolate voice that made the hairs on the back of her neck stand on end. 'And not just as my PA, *cara.*'

Her eyes flew to his, and she caught her breath at the feral hunger gleaming in his green gaze. Tension quivered between them, and the air in the courtyard was so still and silent that Gina was sure he could hear the frantic thud of her heart. 'You shouldn't say things like that,' she whispered. He had broken the unspoken promise between them—not to refer to their mutual awareness of each other—and she felt exposed and vulnerable.

'Why not—when it's the truth?' His arm snaked around her waist and he jerked her up against him, so that she could feel every muscle and sinew of his hard thighs pressing into her softer flesh. 'You must know that I want you,' he said roughly. 'And you want me too. Do you think I don't notice the hungry glances you give me, or the way you trace your lips with your tongue, inviting me to kiss you?'

'I don't—' Gina stopped dead, horrified to realise that she had unconsciously moistened her lips with the tip of her tongue even while Lanzo was speaking. But not because she wanted him to kiss her, she assured herself. Not because she longed for him to cover her mouth with his own and plunder her very soul.

His dark head blotted out the sun, and her heart beat faster as she saw the determined intent in his eyes. She should move, she thought desperately, but her body would not follow the dictates of her brain, and the soft brush of his lips over hers opened the floodgates of desire that she had tried so hard to deny.

Her common sense warned her not to respond, but already it was too late. She had no weapons to fight his sorcery. Her hands were shaking as she placed them against his chest, intending to push him away. The trembling that now affected all her limbs was not from fear, but from a fierce longing to press her body against the muscled strength of his and feel the thud of his heart echo the drumbeat of her own.

Lanzo tasted her again softly, carefully, as if he was aware that she was poised to flee from him. But the gentle pressure of his lips on hers tantalised her senses, and with a low moan she opened her mouth to welcome the erotic sweep of his tongue. And suddenly the dam broke, and he could no longer restrain the thundering torrent of his desire, kissing her with a blazing passion that had her clinging to him while he tangled his fingers in her long, silky hair.

It was Lanzo who finally broke the kiss, the functioning part of his brain reminding him that, although the little courtyard was deserted, they were in full view of the houses surrounding them. He lifted his head reluctantly and frowned. As the head of one of Italy's most successful companies he was a well-known figure in Rome. He never kissed his lovers in public, aware that paparazzi could be lurking anywhere. But yet again Gina had caused him to break one of his personal rules, he thought derisively.

He was unbearably tempted to take her back to his apartment and spend the afternoon making love to her, but once again the wariness in her eyes stopped him. He was sure now that some guy had hurt her in the past. She had brushed off his delicate attempts to probe into her romantic history, but her defensiveness told him there was a reason why she continued to pull back from him. Patience was a virtue, Lanzo reminded himself ruefully. Gina would be his soon, but he would not rush her.

'I leave it up to you to decide what we should do for the rest of the day, *cara*,' he murmured, forcing himself to ease away from her. 'We can go home and relax…' He paused, heat flaring inside him as he imagined removing her shorts and tee shirt and stroking his hands over her voluptuous curves. He took a ragged breath. 'Or we can visit the Pantheon, as we had planned to do.'

Gina stared at him in stunned silence, still reeling from his kiss. Part of her wished that he would make the choice for her, exert his dominance and whisk her back to his apartment so that he could take her to bed for the rest of the day. But she was afraid to admit her longing for him to make love to her. It was more than a step. It was a leap off a precipice. And her nerve failed her.

'I don't want an affair with you,' she said jerkily, cringing at her bluntness but needing to make it clear to him—to herself—that she was not in the market for a sexual fling.

His eyes narrowed, and she saw the effort he made to control his frustration. 'Why not?' he demanded. 'Don't think about denying the chemistry that burned between us when you responded to me so eagerly a few seconds ago. We were good together once,' he reminded her when she shook her head.

'Ten years ago you only wanted me for sex,' Gina reminded him shakily.

'That's not true.' It had started out like that, Lanzo admitted silently. He had been attracted to Gina, but he had assumed that once he had taken her to bed he would soon grow bored with her—as he did with all his mistresses. To his surprise his desire had increased with every week that they had been lovers. He had been drawn to her, and had wanted to spend all his time with her—until alarm bells had rung in his head and he had abruptly ended their affair, determined that he would never allow himself to become emotionally involved with any woman. He had learned that emotions hurt, and he was not prepared to risk going through the pain he had felt when he had lost Cristina ever again.

'It was not just sex. You meant something to me,' he said roughly.

'So much so that I never heard from you again after you returned to Italy?' Gina said bitterly. 'If you cared for me at all—' she could not believe he had '—why didn't you say so?'

'Because my head was messed up.' Lanzo exhaled heavily. 'I wasn't in a fit state of mind to contemplate a relationship. You were young and full of life. You deserved to meet a guy who would make you happy.'

Instead she had met Simon, Gina thought bleakly. 'Why was your head messed up?' she whispered. 'Sometimes I used to glimpse an almost haunted look in your eyes, but you never liked to talk about yourself.' She could tell from his shuttered face that things had not changed and he still would not confide in her. 'I never really knew you at all,' she said sadly. 'And now I don't want to spend a few more weeks as your convenient mistress.'

Lanzo stared at her intently. 'If I only wanted to satisfy a carnal urge there are any number of women I could call,' he said quietly. In truth he did not know exactly what he wanted from a relationship with Gina, but they had been friends as well as lovers ten years ago, and he saw no reason why they could not be so again now. His jaw tightened when he saw panic flare in her eyes. 'What are you afraid of, Gina?'

'I'm not…' The denial died in her throat when he gave her a look of frank disbelief.

'Does your nervousness stem from a previous relationship?' Lanzo voiced what he had begun to suspect, and knew he was near the mark when she quickly looked away from him.

'I don't want to talk about it,' she muttered, stubbornness creeping into her tone. As she pushed her hair back from her face Lanzo noted that her hand was shaking, and a feeling of tenderness swept through him.

'Maybe we both need to open up?' he suggested softly. He wanted to pull her close and simply hold her, until she felt with every beat of his heart that she could trust him. But as he moved towards her she stepped back and shook her head once more.

'What's the point? The only relationship I want with you is as your temporary PA.'

'Look me in the eye and tell me that,' Lanzo ordered, frustrated that he could not understand why she was determined not to give in to the chemistry that was a constant simmering presence between them.

Gina was glad that she had reached into her bag for her sunglasses. She slipped them on and met his gaze calmly, thankful that her expression was hidden from him. 'That's all I want,' she repeated firmly, desperately trying to convince herself as much as him, and before he could say another word she turned and walked out of the courtyard.

There was luxury, and then there was out-of-this-world breathtaking opulence, Gina thought as she stared around in awe at the new Di Cosimo restaurant in St Tropez. Nestled in the hills above the town, it offered diners spectacular views over the bay and the harbour, where huge yachts and motor cruisers—undoubtedly owned by the many multi-millionaires who flocked to the French Riviera during the summer—were moored.

The restaurant was all white marble floors and pillars, with wallpaper flecked with the kind of gold-leaf which also gilded the Louis XV style dining chairs and matched the gold cutlery set out on pristine white linen tablecloths. Stunning centrepieces of white calla lilies and orchids filled the air with their heavenly fragrance, adding to the restaurant's ambience of sumptuous elegance.

'Are you impressed?' Lanzo's deep voice sounded from behind her and she spun round, her breath catching in her throat at the sight of him looking breathtakingly handsome in a formal black dinner suit.

'I'm speechless,' she replied honestly. 'The décor is amazing. And the view from the terrace—those bright pink bougainvillea bushes and beyond them the sapphire-blue sea—is wonderful. I've never seen anything so beautiful.'

'I agree,' Lanzo said softly, not glancing at the view out of the window. Instead his eyes were fixed intently on Gina as he made a slow appraisal of her heather-coloured silk-chiffon dress. Floor-length and strapless, the dress clung to her curves and emphasised her slender waist. She had piled her hair into a chignon with soft tendrils left loose to frame her face, and her only adornment was the rope of pearls that had once been her grandmother's. The smooth, luminescent stones were displayed perfectly against her creamy skin.

'The view from where I'm standing is exquisite,' he murmured, watching dispassionately as soft colour flared along her cheekbones. Since he had kissed her in Rome their relationship had shifted subtly, and the tension between them was tangible. For the past week that they had been in St Tropez, Gina had been excruciatingly polite towards him, perhaps afraid that if they reverted to the easy friendliness they had shared since she had begun to work for him he would think she was willing to have an affair with him.

But despite her coolness Lanzo had been conscious of the fierce sexual chemistry bubbling beneath the surface, waiting to explode. He felt strung out and edgy, his body in a permanent state of arousal—and his patience was at an end. His concentration was shot to pieces, his thoughts dominated by his need to take Gina to bed, and he knew from the way her eyes darkened every time she looked at him that her longing was as great as his.

'Yes, well, everything is ready for the grand opening,' Gina said shakily, dragging her eyes from Lanzo's glinting gaze to glance at her watch. Her senses quivered as she inhaled the subtle scent of his cologne and she took a step away from him, terrified that he would notice her body's betraying reaction to him, her nipples jutting beneath the sheer silk of her gown. 'The guests should start to arrive soon.'

She had barely uttered the words when a sleek black limousine drew up outside the restaurant and moments later a well-known Hollywood star emerged from the car.

The guest list for tonight was chock-full of celebrities, and no expense had been spared to make the launch of the latest Di Cosimo restaurant an event that would hit the headlines around the world. Luisa had begun to organise the launch party before she had gone on maternity leave, but Gina had spent a hectic week finalising arrangements and dealing with last minute problems. Added to that, she had endured four days of the usual agony that accompanied her monthly period. She knew that the painful stomach cramps were a sign that her endometriosis was getting worse, and she was filled with an unbearable sadness that she was unlikely to ever have children.

The only good thing was that she had been so tired and drained at the end of each day that she hadn't had much time to think about Lanzo—although it had been difficult to ignore the escalating sexual tension between them. She did not know what to make of his assertion that he wanted her for more than just sex. If he did not want her for his mistress, what *did* he want? she wondered fretfully. She wished she had the courage to find out, but her marriage and subsequent divorce from Simon had been a bruising experience—and not just mentally, she thought ruefully, her hand straying unconsciously to the scar she had skilfully disguised with make-up. She was afraid to trust her judgement, afraid to give her trust to Lanzo, and now they seemed to be trapped in a strange stalemate which was dominated by their desperate physical awareness of each other.

She was dragged from her thoughts when Lanzo drew her arm through his. 'Duty time,' he murmured when her eyes flew to his face. 'We'll wait at the front entrance to greet the guests as they arrive.'

'Oh, but I thought that as you are the chairman of Di Cosimo Holdings you would prefer to do that on your own. Are you sure you want me…?' Gina trailed to a halt as he gave her an amused smile.

'I'm absolutely certain that I want you, *cara*,' he drawled, his eyes glinting when she blushed scarlet.

The launch party had been a great success, Gina mused hours later, stifling a yawn as she glanced at her watch and saw that it was almost midnight. The food had been divine, accompanied by a selection of the finest wines, and after dinner everyone had strolled out onto the terrace to enjoy the view and the endless supply of champagne served by white-jacketed waiters who wove through the throng of guests.

Inevitably some people had drunk too much—notably an English celebrity television presenter, who regularly featured in the gossip columns and was renowned for his rowdy behaviour. Finn O'Connell had grown increasingly brash and loud-mouthed as the evening progressed. He was swaying unsteadily on his feet, Gina noted, looking over to where Finn was standing with a group of people, including his pretty young wife. Miranda O'Connell was a talented stage actress, and like many people Gina wondered what she saw in her boorish husband.

Gina watched as Finn called to a waiter and demanded another glass of whisky—clearly he had moved on from champagne to neat spirits. His wife put her hand on his arm, as if to plead with him not to have another drink, and Finn reacted explosively, pushing Miranda away with such violence that she stumbled and fell. Gina heard the smash of glass on the tiled floor. As if in slow motion she saw Miranda fall, and memories instantly flooded her mind.

Dear heaven, no—not again, she thought as she flew across the terrace. She pictured Miranda landing on the broken glass, and it brought back the horror of feeling blood pouring in a hot, sticky stream down her own face. Finn O'Connell was shouting at the two burly security guards who had appeared out of the shadows and were gripping his arms. His wife was lying on the floor amid the shards of a broken glass, and Gina could barely bring herself to look, sure that Miranda must have been cut.

Lanzo got there first. He knelt by Miranda's side and spoke to her in a low tone before he gently helped her to her feet. There was no blood, Gina realised with relief. The young actress looked pale and shaken, but seemed otherwise unhurt.

'Stay with Mrs O'Connell while I arrange for a car to take her and her husband back to their hotel,' Lanzo instructed, glancing briefly at Gina. 'I'll tell a waiter to bring her some water—and black coffee for O'Connell,' he added grimly. 'He needs something to sober him up.'

'I'm fine, really,' Miranda said faintly as Lanzo strode away and Gina guided her to a chair. She bit her lip. 'Finn just gets carried away sometimes.'

'Fairly often, if the stories in the tabloids are even half right,' Gina said quietly. When Miranda did not refute this she murmured, 'You're not responsible for the fact that your husband drinks too much. And he has no excuse for lashing out at you—certainly not that he's downed too much whisky.'

Miranda gave her a startled look. 'You sound as though you're speaking from experience.'

Gina nodded. 'I am. Alcohol affects people in different ways; some become happy and relaxed, while others feel morose. My ex-husband used to become bad-tempered and aggressive.' She looked steadily at Miranda. 'I pleaded with Simon to seek help, but he refused to admit he had a problem. When his heavy drinking made him violent I knew that for my safety I had to leave him.' She hesitated, and gave the younger woman a sympathetic smile. 'It's not up to me to tell you how to live your life, but you need to take care of yourself—'

She broke off when Lanzo returned. 'Your car is waiting out front,' he told Miranda. 'I've taken the liberty of sending your husband back to your hotel in a separate car, accompanied by two of my staff. He seems more in control of himself now.' He did not add that Finn O'Connell's bravado had quickly dispersed when he had found himself sharing a car with the two burly bodyguards.

'I hope she'll be okay,' Gina murmured as she and Lanzo watched the hotel manager escort Miranda out of the restaurant.

'The security guards will make sure O'Connell behaves himself for the rest of tonight. Anyway, he's so drunk that he's probably out cold by now. Not that that's an excuse. Any man who hits a woman is a pathetic coward,' Lanzo said disgustedly. He glanced at Gina and frowned. 'Are you all right? You're deathly pale.'

'I'm tired. It's been a long day,' she said hurriedly, desperate to deflect any further questions.

'Go back to the hotel and get to bed. I'll call the driver to take you,' Lanzo said, taking his phone from his jacket. 'I have a few things to finish up here.'

She *was* weary—it hadn't just been an excuse, Gina realised. The upsetting events with Miranda and Finn had been the final straw, and so she did not argue, simply collected her shawl and allowed Lanzo to escort her out to his limousine.

They were staying just outside St Tropez, in a stunning five-star beach-front hotel. Some months ago Luisa had booked the luxurious Ambassador Suite for Lanzo, but she had not made arrangements for any staff who would be accompanying him. When Gina had later phoned the hotel to book a room for herself, and learned that there were no vacancies, she would have been happy to stay at another hotel. But Lanzo had insisted that she should share his suite.

'It has two bedrooms, each with *en suite* bathrooms, as well as an enormous lounge. It's ridiculous for you to stay somewhere else. After all, it won't be any different than us living together in my apartment in Rome,' he'd pointed out when she had tried to argue.

The gleam in Lanzo's eyes had warned Gina of his determination to have his own way, and from a work point of view sharing the suite made sense, she had been forced to admit. But tonight, as she crossed the spacious lounge and entered her bedroom, she locked the door behind her as she had done every night—although whether her actions were to keep Lanzo out or to stop herself from succumbing to temptation and going to him in the middle of the night, she refused to think about.

The night was hot and sultry, and from far out across the

bay came the distant rumble of thunder. Gina opened the French doors, hoping there would be a faint breeze blowing in from the sea, but the air was suffocatingly still.

The scene at the restaurant kept playing over in her mind, but she resolutely pushed it and all its associated memories away as she hung up her dress, washed off her make-up, and slipped a peach silk chemise over her head before she climbed into bed. She had been on her feet since six-thirty that morning, rushing around sorting out last-minute arrangements for the launch party, and she was grateful for the bone-deep weariness that swept over her so that sleep claimed her within minutes.

An hour later Lanzo entered the suite and made straight for the bar, where he poured himself a large brandy. It was his first drink of the night, for although the guests at the party had enjoyed unlimited champagne, he never drank alcohol while he was representing Di Cosimo Holdings. Nursing his glass, he strolled over to the French doors and opened them to step out onto the terrace. The sky was black, lit by neither moon nor stars, and the air prickled with an electricity that warned of an imminent storm.

As he stared out across the dark sea, lightning suddenly seared the sky, ripping through the heavens and illuminating briefly the white wave-crests as they curled onto the shore. His jaw hardened. The day had been intolerably hot and sticky, and hopefully a downpour of rain would clear the air, but he hated storms.

It was ironic that there should be one tonight, he brooded grimly. He hardly needed a reminder that it had been on this date fifteen years ago that lightning had struck his parents' house in Positano and set it ablaze. The fire had been so intense and had spread so quickly that the occupants had not stood a chance. His parents and Cristina had been killed by smoke inhalation while they slept, and when the blaze had finally been brought under control the fire crew had found their bodies still in bed.

He lifted his glass and drained it, feeling the brandy forge a fiery path down his throat. He could no longer see Cristina's face clearly in his mind; time had shrouded her features behind its misty veil and it was now Gina's face, her sapphire-blue eyes and her mouth that tilted upwards at the corners, that was burned onto his brain.

The sound of a cry dragged him from his reverie. It had been a cry of terror—a sharp, frantic cry of mingled fear and pain—and it had come from Gina's room. Pausing only to set his glass down on the table, Lanzo strode swiftly along the terrace, while above him the heavens grumbled menacingly.

CHAPTER SIX

THERE was so much blood. It was hot and wet, pumping all over her white dress and already forming a pool around her head. Gina tossed restlessly beneath the sheet, lost in her dream. She was amazed that she had that much blood, but she needed to stop it pouring out.

With a cry, she jerked upright and pressed her hand to her cheek. It was dark, so dark that she couldn't see, but as the dream slowly ebbed she realised that she wasn't lying on the hard kitchen tiles, and there was no smashed glass beneath her face, no blood seeping from her.

With a shaking hand she fumbled for the switch on the bedside lamp, and at once a soft glow lit up the room. Gina drew a ragged breath. It was a long time since she'd had the dream, and she knew it had been triggered by the events in the restaurant earlier, when Finn O'Connell had pushed his wife and she had fallen, her wine glass shattering on the ground seconds before she had landed. Miranda hadn't been cut, thankfully. But the incident had brought back memories of Simon, drunk and aggressive, hitting her when she tried to take a bottle of whisky from him. The bottle had slipped to the floor, spilling its contents. The smell of whisky still made her feel sick.

Afterwards, Simon had insisted that he hadn't meant to hit her, but whether by accident or design his blow to her temple had been so hard that she had reeled and fallen. She'd been shocked, and she hadn't had time to put out her hands. She had landed on the broken glass, which had sliced through her face and neck.

Pushing back the sheet, she jumped out of bed and fumbled to the open French doors, needing to escape the hot, dark room and the suffocating blackness of her dream. There was no moonlight, and she screamed when she walked into something solid. Hands gripped her arms as she lashed out.

'Gina!' Lanzo spoke her name urgently, shocked by her haunted expression. 'What's the matter, *cara*?'

It was the *cara* that undid her. Lanzo's voice was deep and soft, strength and gentleness meshed, so that she felt instantly safe. She felt instinctively that he would rather die than cause a woman physical harm. He was man of surprisingly old-fashioned values, who opened doors and gave up his seat, and considered it a man's role to protect the weaker sex. Female emancipation was all very well, but at this moment, when she was trembling and felt sick inside, Gina simply allowed him to draw her close and stood silently while he stroked his hand through her hair.

'What happened?' he asked gently.

'Nothing…I had a nightmare, that's all,' she whispered, unable to restrain a shiver as she recalled the details of the dream.

Lanzo gave her a searching glance, feeling a curious little tug in his gut when he saw the shimmer of tears in her eyes. 'Want to talk about it?'

'No.' She swallowed, and tore her eyes from the unexpected tenderness in his.

He sighed and tightened his arms around her, resting his chin on top of her head. No way was he going to allow her to return to her bed alone when she was still clearly upset about her dream. He knew about nightmares. He still suffered from them himself sometimes: tortured images of Cristina, crying out for him amid the flames, and of him unable to save her. He knew what it was like to wake sweating and shaking, afraid to go back to sleep in case the nightmare came again, Lanzo thought grimly.

Gina's hair smelled of lemons. He could not resist the temptation to brush his mouth over her temple, smiling when she gave a jolt but did not try to pull away from him. Gently he trailed his lips down her cheek and over the faint ridge of her scar. She immediately tensed.

'Was your nightmare about the car crash?' he murmured.

Gina drew back a little and gave him a puzzled look. 'What car crash?'

'I assumed you were cut by glass from a shattered windscreen.' It was the only explanation he had been able to think of. 'How *were* you injured, then, *cara*?' He frowned, feeling the tension that gripped her body. Something came into his mind—an image of Gina's terrified face when she had witnessed the incident in the restaurant earlier that night. When Finn O'Connell had lashed out at his wife Gina had looked as shaken as Miranda O'Connell.

A horrific understanding slowly dawned on him. 'Did someone hurt you?' he demanded roughly, feeling sick inside at the possibility. 'Did somebody do this to you, *cara*?'

Gina bit her lip when Lanzo ran his finger lightly down her scar. The compassion evident in his eyes was too much when her nightmare about Simon's brutality was still so real in her head. She felt desperately vulnerable, and her primary instinct was to retreat mentally and physically from Lanzo.

He must have read her mind, for he slid his hand from

her scar to her nape, massaging her tight muscles with a gentle, repetitive motion. 'I would never harm you in any way, *cara*,' he said deeply. 'You must know that.'

She recalled the year she had dated Simon before their marriage, when she'd had no inkling that he had a drink problem and seen no sign of his violent temper. Her wedding night had been memorable for all the wrong reasons, she thought ruefully. Simon had seemed fine after a couple of glasses of champagne at the reception, but on the plane he had ordered spirits, and numerous shots of neat whisky had revealed a side to his personality that had come as an unwelcome shock.

How could you ever know a person's true nature? Gina wondered. And yet she felt safe with Lanzo. She trusted him. And as that realisation sank in relief seeped through her. She had feared she would never feel confident enough to trust anyone again, but Lanzo *was* different from Simon—so different that it was hard to believe they were of the same species.

Lanzo watched the play of emotions on Gina's face, the faint tremor of her mouth before she quickly compressed her lips, and felt a hard knot of anger form in his gut at the idea of some guy hurting her.

'What happened?' he asked quietly, smoothing her hair back from her face and catching her fingers in his when she instinctively tried to cover the thin, slightly raised ridge that he had exposed.

She was under no obligation to tell him anything—so why did she feel a strong urge to share the memories that still had the power to evoke nightmares? He was so tall that she had to tilt her head to look at his face, and as she studied his hard jaw a wry smile tugged her lips. Strength and undeniable power meshed with the gentle expression in his eyes were a potent combination. She felt safe with Lanzo; it was as simple as that.

But it was still hard to admit the truth. Gina took a shaky breath. 'My husband…did this,' she said huskily. 'He was in one of his rages and he hit me.'

For a few stark seconds Lanzo went rigid with shock. 'You're *married*?' he demanded harshly.

'Not any more.' She managed a ghost of a smile that did not reach her eyes. 'My divorce was finalised just before I moved back to Poole, but I *had* left Simon a year before that. The night he did this—' she touched her scar '—was the final straw. I knew I had to get away from him before anything worse happened.'

'*Dio mio,*' Lanzo growled. 'How on earth did you end up married to such a monster in the first place?'

Gina bit her lip. It was a question that the few close friends who knew what had happed during her marriage had asked her. She felt a fool that she had been duped by Simon, and it was hard for her to talk about her marriage, but she acknowledged that she was never going to be able to move forward with her life until she had come to terms with her past.

'Simon was an investment banker. We met at a corporate dinner in the City,' she explained wearily. 'He was good-looking, charming, and successful—I guess he ticked all the right boxes, and we quickly became close. We were engaged six months after we met, and married six months after that. Our wedding night was the first time I had ever seen him drunk, but the next morning he was so apologetic that I put it down to the stress of the wedding.'

She sighed. 'Making excuses for Simon's drinking and his black moods became a regular occurrence, but I wanted our marriage to work and so I kept on ignoring the warning signs of his increasing reliance on alcohol.'

'I don't understand how you could have ignored it if he was violent towards you,' Lanzo said harshly. It struck him that Gina must have been madly in love with her husband to put up with his behaviour, and he was unprepared for the sharp stab of jealousy in his gut that the thought evoked.

Gina could see the shock in Lanzo's eyes and she hung her head, moving away from him to stare out of the window at the dark beach. 'I was ashamed,' she admitted in a low tone. 'I thought that I must somehow be to blame for Simon's drinking and his tempers. And I didn't know who to talk to. We were part of a large social group, but most of the people we met at dinner parties were Simon's business associates and I couldn't possibly have confided to any of them or their sophisticated wives that we were not the glamorous have-it-all couple we appeared to be.'

She twisted her fingers together, still not able to look at Lanzo. 'I know I was a fool, but I was clinging to my dream of having a family. We had agreed to try for a child as soon as we were married, and I hoped that a baby would magically make Simon stop drinking. Instead, I failed to fall pregnant, Simon lost his job in the banking crisis that hit the City, and things went rapidly from bad to awful because he spent all day at home drowning his sorrows.'

'Yet you still stayed with him?'

'I wanted to help him. I felt guilty that I didn't love the man he had turned into, but I was still his wife, and I felt it was my duty to try and support him. The trouble was Simon didn't want to be helped. During one of our many rows about his drinking I tried to take his bottle of whisky, and he reacted like a madman.' She swallowed, the memories vivid in her mind. 'He struck me, and as I fell I dropped the bottle I was holding. A piece of broken glass sliced through my face, and by unlucky chance through an artery in my neck. There was a lot of blood and confusion.